Bliss Bonner Was Stunned— Absolutely Shattered!

Whatever she had expected, it had not been this cold, calculated attack on her brother as a person.

"I've spoken to my sister and to your brother more than once," he said tightly. "He is *not* to call, *not* to try to get her to meet him, and if there's any more bother on that score, I'll see that he gets more trouble than he ever bargained for. I won't have my sister wasting herself on a chap who'll probably end up doing time!"

"Is that *quite* all, Mr. Etchison?" Bliss made herself reply.

He stood up, his lean, rugged frame under the flawless evening clothes somehow threatening. His voice was as impersonal as his touch. "That's all."

DIXIE BROWNING
grew up on Hatteras Island off the coast of North Carolina. She is an accomplished and well-known artist of watercolors, as well as a prolific writer.

Dear Reader:

Silhouette Books is pleased to announce the creation of a new line of contemporary romances—*Silhouette Special Editions*. Each month we'll bring you six new love stories written by the best of today's authors—Janet Dailey, Brooke Hastings, Laura Hardy, Sondra Stanford, Linda Shaw, Patti Beckman, and many others.

Silhouette Special Editions are written with American women in mind; they are for readers who want more: more story, more details and descriptions, more realism, and more *romance*. *Special Editions* are longer than most contemporary romances allowing for a closer look at the relationship between hero and heroine with emphasis on heightened romantic tension and greater sensuous and sensual detail. If you want more from a romance, be sure to look for *Silhouette Special Editions* on sale this February wherever you buy books.

We welcome any suggestions or comments, and I invite you to write us at the address below.

Karen Solem
Editor-in-Chief
Silhouette Books
P.O. Box 769
New York, N. Y. 10019

DIXIE BROWNING
Winter Blossom

Silhouette *Romance*

Published by Silhouette Books New York

America's Publisher of Contemporary Romance

Other Silhouette Romances by Dixie Browning

East of Today
Journey to Quiet Waters
Tumbled Wall
Unreasonable Summer
Wren of Paradise

SILHOUETTE BOOKS, a Simon & Schuster Division of
GULF & WESTERN CORPORATION
1230 Avenue of the Americas, New York, N.Y. 10020

Copyright © 1981 by Dixie Browning

Distributed by Pocket Books

ISBN: 0-671-57113-3

First Silhouette Books printing November, 1981

10 9 8 7 6 5 4 3 2 1

America's Publisher of Contemporary Romance

Printed in the U.S.A.

Chapter One

Bliss eyed the shell-pink satin gown with distaste. She considered the possibility of removing the wine stain near the hem and decided with relief that it was there to stay. One more outfit scratched from the never-ending list. Honestly, sometimes she felt like Morton's doll with the way he delighted in dressing her up and parading her around for everyone to see!

She reached for her favorite denim wraparound skirt and a soft cotton blouse that owed its privileged place in her voluminous wardrobe more to comfort than to fashion. Tossing the ruined satin aside, she shimmied into a pair of panty hose and whipped the skirt around her tiny waist.

An unnatural child, he called her, because she would much prefer that he gave her the lovely porphyry urn for the garden than yet another of the exotic creations from his Mayfair shop. But to Bliss's way of thinking, there was nothing at all unnatural in preferring to spend her afternoon muddling about in the garden, with its lovely scent of humus, flowers and herbs, instead of perched uncomfortably on a tiny gilt chair inhaling cigarette smoke and heavy perfume while a dozen gaunt clotheshorses strode arrogantly up and down the runway, flaunting Reynaldo's newest creations. Reynaldo hated having to adapt his things to Bliss's too small, too voluptuous figure and he didn't mind letting her know it. But it was Morton's shop and Reynaldo had only been what he termed an altar boy for one of the lesser shops off Oxford Road when Morton had hired him to do alterations and discovered his flair for design.

That flair had made the small shop, Chez Henri, rise above its modest beginnings. Now it offered Reynaldo's original line along with Morton's exclusive selection of women's wear. There were still times when Morton failed to appreciate the irony of having his own ward dressed in clothes that might have come from a jumble sale.

By the time Bliss reached the breakfast table, Morton had already left. The scent of coffee preceded Martha as the plump housekeeper shouldered her way through the baize doors with the percolator, a rack of toast and a pot of marmalade. Bliss shoved the morning paper aside; it had been laid at her place, anchored by a heavy silver saltshaker, and only as she moved it did she notice the photograph in the upper left-hand corner.

"Oh, blast," she muttered as she ate her toast, tilting the picture so that she could read the caption: "Morton Henry of Chez Henri puts his seal of approval on his lovely young protégée." She read the rest of the gossip column derisively, wondering who would be faintly interested in a middle-aged businessman who was celebrating a business deal with his ward. The sketchy article failed to mention the fact that she had been in Morton's care since she was fourteen, and that they were toasting the success of an agreement he had just signed with an American manufacturer to distribute a moderately priced line of the Chez Henri originals under a new label.

The photographer had caught them just as Morton, his arm draped casually across Bliss's bare shoulders, planted a kiss on her cheek. Their champagne glasses had been held high, and, as usual with that sort of sloppy journalism, the whole thing was open to misinterpretation. Protégée, indeed! Benji might qualify for the term, for he at least worked for Morton, but as far as Bliss herself was concerned, assistant housekeeper and gardener's helper might come closer to the mark!

Not that it mattered, she supposed. Who would read it except for Benji or, perhaps, Reade? And they both knew what a lot of malarkey it was. On the plus side, it just might reinforce the defenses Morton had cultivated so carefully over the years. Being wealthy, unattached and extremely presentable, even at forty-six, could be a hazard when one employed a crew of glamorous and sometimes opportunistic females, not to mention a female manager who would give her next year's Givenchy to become Mrs. Morton Henry.

Martha returned with a boiled egg and a plate of fruit. "All right, Bliss, you're going to have to finish this off if you hope to keep up with those painters this morning. I heard you come in just before the milkman and I'll not have you running yourself ragged on a piece of toast and three cups of coffee."

She stood over her to see that the plate was

7

polished clean, just as she had been doing ever since a silent, lost girl of fourteen and her eighteen-year-old brother were left unexpectedly in the care of their only relative, a cousin they had never met, when their parents had been lost in a sailing accident. It had been Martha who had held Bliss together in her plump, warm arms then, and the middle-aged housekeeper had been guiding her ever since.

"Hmph! So you saw that nasty picture Mr. Morton left open for you. That dress! You'd think he'd have better sense than to take you out in public looking like one of his fancy women from the shop. But then, what man has a grain of sense when it comes to what's right for a woman to wear?"

"Martha, that's rank heresy and you know it." Bliss laughed.

"Oh, I'm not saying you didn't look a picture in it, mind you. But a man that age ought to know better than to doll you up in a frock that's cut all the way down to your goozle!"

Bliss stifled a giggle. She had long pondered the location of that precise bit of anatomy. Whenever she wore a dress whose neckline Martha disapproved of, it was cut all the way *down* to the goozle; but if it was a skirt that was slit too drastically, then it was cut all the way *up* to her goozle. As nearly as she could figure it, the moot part must be somewhere around her waist.

"It was a bit drafty, but then, it was designed for someone like Stella, or that new model, the one with the haircut . . . what's her name?" Bliss helped herself to another cup of coffee.

"As if I knew one of them females from another.

8

If you ask me, they all look more like lampposts than they do women!''

Which was little less than the truth, as Morton's mannequins tended to go to extremes which focused the attention on Chez Henri rather than reflecting on the women who bought his creations. Few of those creations were designed to flatter women of Bliss's tiny but well rounded build. The pink satin had looked stunning on the narrow five feet ten inches of the regular model. But with a generous amount taken off the bottom to accommodate Bliss's five feet three inches, and enough added to the top to cover her generous bosom, it had been quite another thing altogether. It flattered her ivory complexion and her heavy waves of chestnut hair, as Morton had promised her it would. It highlighted what he called her incandescent eyes, which were a perfectly ordinary light brown. But it also managed to show quite an expanse of creamy cleavage, and that was what the news photo zeroed in on, to her chagrin.

"Did you see the other picture?" the house-keeper asked now, indicating the bottom fold of the paper. "That boy! He needs a hand applied where it would do the most good, if you ask me!" At twenty-four Benji was still "that boy" to Martha Biggam.

With a feeling of dread, Bliss held the smaller photo so that it caught the light. It showed a group of uninhibited youngsters gyrating at a new disco. It could have been worse, even though the caption mentioned the trouble police had had with this and other, similar places. Of course, there in the middle, dressed in the jeans and beaded vest he favored when he was not at work, was Benji, grinning broadly, with a drink in one hand and a girl in the other—a tiny thing who looked as if she should be home doing her schoolwork.

Oh, drat! At twenty-four, her brother showed no more of a tendency to grow up than he had at eighteen. Morton was doing his best, exercising a patience Bliss often marveled at and giving him a job at Chez Henri in the accounting department. Benji's one outstanding talent was with figures . . . of all sorts—a comment he added with a wink whenever the subject came up.

It would have done him no harm to have gone to the club with her and Morton to celebrate the signing of the papers. Almost everyone concerned was there. But no, he had to go running after a wide-eyed little teenager!

The painters came and Bliss saw them established before spending half an hour with Morton's social calendar, answering a few invitations and ordering flowers for the weekend. She joined Martha in the kitchen, went over the menu with her and then put on her gardening gloves and rewarded herself with an hour or two at her very favorite occupation, thus clearing away the remnants of last night's smoky, noisy atmosphere. There was nothing she enjoyed so much as working—or even just sitting and day-dreaming—in Morton's small but beautifully de-signed garden.

The painters finally left and Bliss set about putting the rooms back together again. She was up on a ladder hanging the newly aired draperies when the phone rang, and a few minutes later Martha called upstairs to say that Morton would be flying to New York tonight. He would be home for tea and would have just enough time to throw a few things into a bag.

Bliss would have liked to do more than mention the article in the paper as they finished a quick tea; then she had half decided not to bring up the subject at all. There was nothing Morton could do to curb her brother's increasingly wild behavior anyway, and it wasn't fair to burden him now with this new venture hardly off the ground.

"You saw the papers, I take it," he said, finishing a second cup of tea as he took the matter out of her hands.

"Yes."

"Etchison will have his scalp if that young man doesn't watch his step. I understand he's been having even more trouble with that kid sister of his than we have with Benji."

"You mean the girl in the photo? She hardly looked the sort," Bliss observed, loading the tray to save Martha the steps. "You know them, then?"

"Know *him*. Lombard Street type . . . handled our end of the MacHenry thing. His firm backed us substantially, and I hate like the very devil for that young cub to throw a spanner in the works. Here, hold my coat, there's a dear." He handed her the handsomely tailored chesterfield and shifted his briefcase while she eased the coat over his shoulders.

"You look lovely," she told him. "No wonder I can't look at another man." He did, too, she thought fondly, admiring the way his white sideburns contrasted with his carefully cultivated year-round tan.

Two nights later Bliss was in the bath when the phone rang. As Martha was out and Benji had just left, Bliss muttered a mild oath and stepped soapy from the tub, grabbing a towel and hurrying to the upstairs extension.

It was Morton and he told her that he was going to be in the States at least a couple of days longer than he had planned and to have Benji inform the staff. Then he went on to give her more particular orders to be relayed to certain associates, explaining that his secretary was absent for a few days and couldn't be reached.

"Take care of yourself, Morton, and don't forget to take your vitamins. You tend to run yourself ragged on these trips," Bliss reminded him fondly.

"Yes, Mother," he mocked in reply. There was a bond of deep affection between them and Bliss half suspected it had something to do with her own mother, whom she resembled more all the time.

Before she could lower herself back into her rapidly cooling tub, the doorbell rang and this time her oath was not quite so mild as she snatched up her peach silk robe and struggled to pull it on over her still-damp body. Her scatterbrained brother forgot his keys half the time. For all his skill at maths, Benji was an aggravating scamp who unfortunately had about as much common sense as a pet rabbit!

"All right, all right," she cried impatiently as the bell rang again. She snatched open the paneled door, words of remonstrance on her lips, only to be confronted by a perfect stranger. Her first instinct was to slam the door in his face, and she had actually made the first move, one hand clutching her robe at the neck while the other tightened on the polished brass knob, when he forestalled her.

"I want to see Morton Henry," the man announced. No "please," no "if it's convenient," no nothing!

"I'm sorry," Bliss replied repressively, "but Morton's . . ." And then she came to her senses. She was all alone in the house, with the nearest neighbor separated by two walled gardens—too far away for comfort in the face of this cold, intimidating stranger.

"I'm sorry, Mr. Henry can't be disturbed just now," she amended haughtily. "If you'd care to leave your card . . ."

"Then I'll just have to wait until he does feel like being disturbed," the man said imperturbably, pushing his way inside as if she weren't even there.

"You can't come in here!" Bliss exploded. "I'll call the—"

"Go right ahead, miss." His eyes raked her disparagingly as he stepped deeper into the marble-floored foyer and closed the door behind him. "Call whomever you like. The sooner we get this matter resolved, the better I'll like it." His tone of voice said he had better things to do than waste time with a go-between, and Bliss began to simmer as her fear was replaced by indignation. Her chestnut hair was only one shade removed from red and her temper had a slightly lower than average boiling point, as well. She was certainly too volatile to allow this ill-bred creature his own way. She marched to the fruitwood hunt table and picked up the phone. Even as her finger touched the dial, she found her wrist encircled by a sinewy manacle.

"Unless you're calling Morton Henry, I'd advise you to put down the phone." His voice was as cold as a killing frost. "My business won't take up more than a few minutes of his time, so I'm sure you can get along without him for that long," he sneered.

Refusing to be intimidated, Bliss lifted her chin and stared at him coolly. "If you'd care to leave a message, I'll see that he gets it."

"My business has to do with that young pup, Bonner. I intend to put my point across face to face so there'll be no mistake."

A heavy weight settled in Bliss's chest as she slowly pulled her wrist from his crippling grip, rubbing it unconsciously with her other hand. Benji! She might have known he couldn't go a whole month without winding up in trouble. Torn between wanting to see the back of this unpleasant man and wanting to know the extent of Benji's predicament, she bit her lip and frowned at the stranger.

He was about thirty-five or so, she surmised, and quietly but extremely well dressed in a dark gray suit. He had the sort of face one would hate to have to deal with from a witness stand, although some women might argue that point, she conceded grudgingly. But then, across a candlelit table he might be more approachable. His features were really rather stunning in a lean, hawkish way. But at the moment the gray of his eyes, like the gray that lightly frosted his thick, dark hair, reminded her of ice.

"I assure you, miss, that I'm not interested in the family silver, nor in your . . . 'virtue,' either." That last was in definite quotes, with an insulting lift of his supercilious brows. She glared at him, unable to cope with such blatant malice, especially as she hadn't the faintest idea what had prompted it.

"Would you mind telling me exactly who you are and what your business with Mr. Henry concerns, other than Mr. Bonner?" she asked. Her voice had dwindled in force as she underwent his raking scrutiny.

"The name is Etchison and my business is personal!"

"Well, Mr. Etchison, I'm afraid you'll have to be more explicit than that before I can—"

He interrupted her. "Is Henry here or not?"

"Mr. Henry is not available at the moment," she replied grimly.

"Then you may inform Mr. Henry that I'll see him in his office at nine-thirty in the morning," he announced witheringly, turning to let himself out before Bliss could so much as move. He closed the door behind him with controlled fury, leaving her to stalk upstairs to a completely cold bath.

During the several hours she lay awake, Bliss rehearsed the many things she would have liked to say to the man. Why was it these gems never popped into her head until long after the moment had passed? Her easygoing nature always prevailed far too long during any confrontation. Then, when she would finally boil over, it would invariably be too late to get off any really telling blows because the enemy had by that time retreated.

In this case, retreat was hardly the word. In this case, too, her good nature had hardly had time to come into play. As soon as the door had closed behind him, Bliss remembered where she had heard the name, and it had been in a context guaranteed to keep her lying awake far into the night.

She would love to be a fly on the wall tomorrow when Morton's office dragon, Miss Scourby, told him that Mr. Henry was not in and would not be in for several days. Let him cool his well-shod heels for a little while, she thought with a drowsy grin.

It was unfortunate that she overslept the next morning. She had scheduled a very early appointment to have a molar filled, not her favorite way to start the day. After that, she would have to run by the shop to see if Benji had showed up, because Martha had greeted her with the news that his bed had not been slept in. It wasn't the first time, by any means, and he always resented her prying into his affairs. But all the same, she felt years older than her errant brother, and a combination of concern and irritation kept her after him whenever he stepped too far out of line.

It was past nine when she left the dentist's, her jaw aching abominably as the numbness began to wear off. She still had to go by the shop before meeting the plasterer about the dining-room ceiling. Leaving her Mini in the parking space reserved for Morton a few minutes later, she ducked out and ran, head bent against the persistent drizzle. She had just jumped a puddle when she careened into something hard and unyielding.

"Whoops! Better watch it unless . . . *you!*" the man exclaimed.

"Oh, sorry," Bliss apologized breathlessly, hearing her own voice as it slurred over the words. She was well aware of how she must look as he held her by the arms and glared down at her accusingly, taking in every detail of her pale, cosmetic-free face.

Well, who could put lipstick on a numb mouth? She knew better than to even try, and besides, what was she doing thinking of how she looked when the contemptuous Mr. Etchison was glaring down at her as if she had just crawled out from under a rock?

She jerked her arms away and returned his glare full measure. "I suppose you've been trying to see Morton again," she jeered, muttering an "oh, darn" under her breath as her tongue tried and failed to enunciate her words clearly.

"Quite right," he retorted curtly, "but after seeing you last night and this morning as well, I can tell I may as well be patient until the celebration is over." His thick black eyebrows lifted disdainfully in his harsh face as he nodded briefly and strode across the lot to slide under the wheel of a low, black Maserati.

She was still standing there, seething impotently, as he swerved out into the midmorning traffic with controlled impatience.

She smiled at Max, who served as doorman, delivery man and occasional chauffeur, crossed the muted taupe carpet with a word here and there to the sales staff and closed the wrought-iron doors of the lift with a sigh of relief. Benji was in his cluttered office on the second floor, and when the maid told her that he was going over some figures with Mr. Ketchum and would be tied up for ages, she was actually relieved. She used the ladies' room, trying with some success to apply a touch of color to her face before going on to her next appointment, all the while telling herself she was being cowardly to put off talking to Benji.

Of course, she was glad to know that he hadn't wrapped his red sports car around a lamppost and ended up in a hospital, nor had he landed himself in jail, both very real considerations where her irresponsible brother was concerned. All the same, she would have to give him a talking to for worrying Martha that way. He might at least have called if he had planned to be out all night.

On her way to the lift again, she came face to face with the subject of her worries when Benji stepped out into the corridor for another cup of black coffee. "All right, Benji, what's the excuse this time?" she asked tiredly, nursing her sore jaw.

"Uh-oh! Sorry, sis," the almost too good-looking young man said. "I had a snootful last night and it didn't seem to be a smart idea to drive home in that condition." He eyed her speculatively, as if to see how his excuse went down. Then, seeing her skepticism, he went on. "It's true, Bliss. Honest! It was a pretty freewheeling party and there was a lot of stuff going down, but at least I had the sense to stick to good old basic alcohol. Better the devil you know, and all that." He tried a grin that wavered and died.

Honestly, how could one cope with a case like this? She probed her tender tooth with an exploratory tongue and tried a new tack. "There was a man named Etchison trying to see Morton last night and again this morning. Would you happen to know anything about it?"

He flushed a dull red and avoided her eyes. "I suppose he saw the pic in the paper yesterday. It's a little matter of his sister, see? Old James doesn't happen to share your exalted opinion of one Benjamin Arthur Bonner the third."

"Exalted, my foot! What about his sister, Benji?"

"If you must know, I've been seeing a bit of her. She's a neat kid and, believe it or not, I . . . well, I rather fancy her. So-o-o, big brother got himself in a lather and threatened my hide if I so much as looked at her again." He spoke airily, but Bliss could tell that he was not as blasé as he pretended.

"When was this?"

"Oh . . . last week. At least, that was the last time," he added with a sick grin.

She got it out of him bit by bit, hating herself for having to be in that position and hating Benji for putting her there. It seemed that her wild brother had fallen for a girl whose family had other plans for her and objected vociferously to her running around with someone they considered a wastrel. The fact that her family was loaded and Benji was almost always in debt might have something to do with that, Bliss decided grimly.

"Was that the child you were . . . wriggling with in the news photo?" she asked resignedly, causing him to throw back his head and laugh.

"Honestly, Bliss, anyone would think you were my maiden aunt instead of my kid sister. Wriggling! I don't suppose you and Reade ever go beyond a sedate waltz. But yes, that was Leigh I was wriggling with. Cute, isn't she? She's a pretty nice person, too, even if her brother does come down on her like a ton of bricks."

"James Etchison is her brother? What about her father? What does he have to say about it?"

"Oh, they're a matched pair, like we are. Just the two of them, although if I tried to clamp down on you the way James does on poor Leigh, you'd have my head . . . not that you've ever done anything wilder than plant tomatoes in the rose garden."

"Thanks," she sniffed. She rather resented being thought so hopelessly dull, even if there was more truth than poetry to his remarks.

"Look, Bliss, I really do like this girl. I may even

19

love her, I don't know. The thing is, how can I ever find out if that old bas—— . . . excuse me. But honestly, he keeps her shut up in the castle with the moat bridge up and . . ." He shrugged his shoulders, looking young and miserable.

"How old is she?" Bliss asked more gently.

"Uh . . . almost eighteen," he admitted hesitantly.

"Oh, my sainted aunt," his sister groaned. "Benji, she's a child! No wonder her brother is worried about her. You aren't exactly the most circumspect soul around, you know. If I weren't your sister . . ."

"All right, all right! At any rate, he has no business going to Morton behind my back, and that's what he said he was going to do if I ever tried to see her again." He looked at her in a way that brought out her maternal instinct, even though she knew she should have sorted him out good. Honestly, how could she deal with a brother who, by all rights, should have been looking after her instead of the other way around?

By the time she got there, the plasterer was out on another job and she was told to come back to see him before ten the next morning for an estimate. She made her way home, secretly glad she had not had to get involved in the repairs of the damaged plaster in the dining-room ceiling. It was one of three ornate molded ones in the house and she knew it was going to cost a bundle to replace it.

The interview with Benji nagged at her as she eased her three-year-old Mini out into Park Lane traffic. On determining that he had deliberately gone against the girl's brother's wishes, she was tempted to let him face the music alone. It seemed the only way he might learn a lesson, but the girl looked awfully young. Perhaps she deserved something better than the all too charming but hopelessly irresponsible Benji. Bliss loved her brother dearly, but long before their parents went down aboard the *Ariel*, she had recognized the fact that, as the only son, he was shamefully indulged.

As she considered the feasibility of leaving him to the not too tender mercies of James Etchison, the focus of her thoughts shifted. A more unpleasant individual she had yet to meet, she decided grimly as she parked the Mini and hurried under the dripping plane trees into the tall, narrow house, with its black wrought iron and front door gleaming wetly against the pristine white facade.

The vision that went with her, however, was not of a pair of frigid gray eyes blazing down at her with contempt, nor of a long, wedge-shaped back that looked as though it would break before it bent. All she could call to mind was his mouth that was both firm and sensual, and his thick, dark hair in which rain and silver both crystallized like frost.

Chapter Two

By the time Morton returned from New York five days later, Bliss had all but forgotten her worries about Benji and his affairs. The newly redone bedrooms awaited her cousin's inspection, and she felt quite proud of the work she had done on them. The lovely old house had not been refurbished since Morton's mother's day, and Mrs. Henry had died two years before the young Bonners had come to live there with Morton and his housekeeper.

She had done a thorough job on Morton's study while he had been gone, carefully putting it back together again just as she had found it; then she had spent every sunny moment she could spare in the garden, clearing away the spent annuals and taking up tender bulbs.

Meanwhile, Benji had behaved in an exemplary manner, even going so far as to take her out to dinner on a night when he hadn't had a date. Bliss managed to assure herself that the girls he was seeing were old enough to fend for themselves in the face of his rather unfair advantages in the way of looks and personal charm. Otherwise, she saw little of him as she scribbled on notepads her plans for making the most of the winter bloomers, the *Viburnum fragans*, the *Daphne mezereum* and the wintersweet and heliotrope.

Morton arrived home triumphant, having brought off what he considered a great coup. "Of course, MacMurdle is busy congratulating himself, as well. Fact is, my dear, we both landed on top of the heap."

Bliss was interested, naturally, since both Morton and Benji's future hinged on the success of Chez Henri and its new offshoot, MacHenry, Inc. She was far more interested, though, in domestic things, a fact Benji deplored and one to which Morton reluctantly resigned himself. After all, she reassured herself, the upholstery course she had taken so that she could redo the dining-room chairs would produce something that lasted far longer than any of the exotic creations in which Morton dealt. Fashion went out almost before it was really in, but fine furniture, a well-run, well-appointed home—those things gave so much satisfaction; they had a lasting effect on the people who lived there, and it gave her immense pleasure to think she had a small part in it all.

It occurred to her, not for the first time, that her present attitude might be a reaction to a childhood spent in boarding schools and vacations spent wherever her gypsylike parents happened to be sailing at the time.

A week after Morton had returned from the States he phoned from the shop to ask Bliss to meet him for lunch at the Connaught. In the middle of putting up pear conserve, she hesitated.

"It's important, dear, or I wouldn't have torn you away from your warm hearth," he assured her.

"Oh, that's all right, Morton. Martha can finish up for me and I'll meet you at . . . did you say one? Shall I pick you up?"

"No need. Max will drop me off when he delivers the Florence models and you can bring me back afterward if you will."

It was just after one when Bliss, flushed and tense after a late start and a traffic fray involving a limo and a delivery van, entered the handsome country-mansion-style hotel and made her way to the restaurant. The understated elegance, as always, had a soothing effect on her as she was ushered to a table where two men and one small girl watched her approach.

"Bliss, this is Leigh Etchison and her brother, James. James, Leigh—Bliss Bonner." Morton made the introductions while Bliss stared dumbly into the cool, evaluating eyes of the man who extended his hand to her.

She touched it automatically, then jerked back her own hand and turned to the girl, who was staring with an openness that fell just short of rudeness. Leigh Etchison was quite beautiful, or at least she would be once she had outgrown a certain petulance. She was obviously irritated about something and made no effort to hide the fact, raking Bliss with her derisive blue eyes before turning back to her drink. Like brother, like sister, Bliss thought wryly, settling into the chair Morton held for her.

"I hope you'll forgive our intrusion, Miss Bonner," James Etchison remarked indifferently, as if he really didn't care one way or another. "My sister and I were about to order when Morton came in and I didn't realize when we invited him to join us that you'd be meeting him."

She smiled with saccharine sweetness. In other words, she thought rancorously, if he had known, neither Bliss nor Morton would have been allowed in their exalted presence. In a pig's eye!

She answered whenever a direct question was put to her, but otherwise she concentrated on the *briouate*, a succulent meat-stuffed pastry, and a *salade*. Five minutes afterward, she couldn't have named a single item she had consumed.

Leigh only toyed with her food as she shot her brother smoldering glances, to which he seemed completely impervious. He and Morton talked mostly of the red tape involved in overseas operations, and Bliss was allowed the freedom to examine the man at close range. She was toying with her wineglass as she wondered if the intimidating aura that hovered about him had to do with the ease with which he wore his finely tailored clothes, as if they were as comfortable to him as her denim and jerseys were to her. Or was it more to do with the perfect control he maintained over those angular features of his? She would hate to find herself in an argument with someone like that; he was utterly impervious, and it showed.

"Well, Bliss, I didn't drag you out today just to feed you," Morton announced, turning to smile at her.

"I assumed as much," she replied, with a warm grin of her own.

"You see, I've been putting in my two bits about the image we're trying to promote, and while Mac-

Murdle agrees that the London scene is important, he insists that we steer clear of the typical high-fashion types and use someone the American public can identify with." He grimaced as he tapped a cigarette against a flat silver case. "I'm afraid he thinks we'll reek of Carnaby in its heyday," he admitted.

"Why not use their own models?" Bliss asked reasonably.

"For one thing, they want totally new faces. For another, I want to put together a portfolio using my own ideas . . . nothing final, you understand. But I think . . . I just believe they may go for it. Which is where you come in."

"You've done some modeling before, Miss Bonner?" James asked with a politeness that bordered on ennui.

Determined not to allow herself to fly off the handle, Bliss answered, "No, Mr. Etchison, I haven't. In fact, my brother . . . oh, have you met Benji yet?" Her wide-eyed look of innocence accompanied the query and she continued without waiting for a reply. "Benji says I'm more turboprop than jet set. But if Morton needs me, of course I'll be glad to do whatever I can."

She had the pleasure of seeing the frost thaw slightly as what might have been a glint of amusement flashed through his narrowed gray eyes.

"You'll have to put up with considerable discomfort, I'm afraid, love, while Reynaldo does his last-minute alterations. But if you'll do the evening wear, there's a new creature at the Channing agency, just come from Sweden, I think, and hardly known anywhere yet. It occurs to me that she might be just the thing to do the sportswear. She has those long legs, yards of white hair flying about and all that."

"Sounds possible, but I'm afraid we're boring your friends, Morton. We can talk it over tonight after you get home." It wasn't any of their concern, and besides, it wasn't like Morton to be discussing a publicity campaign with perfect strangers; those things were classified information in the Mayfair district.

"Oh, James is very much in the picture, darling. I told you his firm has been underwriting this venture from the first, didn't I?"

Feeling a trickle of cold run down her spine that was only partly due to the dry satisfaction on James's face as he smiled tightly at her, Bliss subsided. She hated the idea of any connection whatsoever between her and this man. That Benji was involved with his sister was bad enough, but if he was up to his well-trimmed sideburns in the affairs of Chez Henri, then it would be impossible to avoid occasional contact. And she had the dreadful feeling that any contact at all would be to her detriment.

"I thought you understood, my dear," Morton was saying when she refocused her attention. "Benji knows, of course, being in the bookkeeping department. But you stay all wrapped up in that cozy little cocoon you've woven for yourself and half of what I say sails right over your pretty little head."

"Oh, Morton, you make me sound so dense." Bliss laughed ruefully, reaching for her purse and gloves as a hint that she would like to end this uncomfortable meeting. Uncomfortable! That was an understatement!

"Not at all, child, but you must know that the days of haute couture are waning rapidly. Inflation, world tensions, changing values . . . these things hit the luxury trade where it hurts, and I'm counting on the MacHenry thing to put us back into the picture."

Bliss looked directly at the young girl, who sat slumped over, toying idly with a spoon, while she sighed in obvious boredom. "It might be possible to use Miss Etchison for some of the things, Morton. The young set needs—"

She wasn't allowed to finish. "Unfortunately, my sister will be unable to take part in anything of that sort," James remarked austerely. "She'll be visiting friends in Cornwall for the next few months."

So that was it, Bliss thought. That's what's behind all the heavy sighs and the murderous looks the poor child has been shooting his way.

It was Morton who made the first move to leave, after glancing impatiently at his wafer-thin gold watch. He turned to the Etchisons apologetically and said, "I'm afraid I must dash, Leigh, James. I wanted to stop by the Channing Agency, and then there's this fabric fellow over near Russell Square . . . I'll have to let Bliss drop me by the shop and take Max, I suppose."

Goodbyes were perfunctory after that, as everyone seemed to have private concerns. On the way back to the shop, Morton seemed lost in thought and it took all Bliss's concentration to negotiate traffic. Just before she pulled over to let him out, Morton murmured that James had mentioned wanting to talk to him about something and that they had never gotten around to it. "Oh, well, I suppose if it's important, he'll be in touch. Thanks, love. I may run late this evening, but I'll be in for dinner."

"It's important, all right," Bliss muttered to herself as she headed home, only maybe now that the problem was being taken care of by shipping his precious sister out of harm's way, perhaps the Bonners and the Etchisons could leave one another in peace. By the time Leigh got back to town, Benji would have gone through half a dozen girls. As for James's involvement with Chez Henri, if it had gone on all this time without her even being aware of it, then it was probably just a paper partnership and she needn't worry about bashing heads with him again.

The next three weeks were crammed with activity as almost everyone seemed to be doing ten different things at once. Bliss, in the midst of making apple butter and putting up fruit for future tarts, as well as mulching the more tender inhabitants of the garden, was called on time and time again to dash into town. She hated to have to stand still for hours while Reynaldo and his minions pinned, poked and prodded at her, all the while discussing her as if she were an inanimate object: "The bust is much too high . . . the waist is impossible! No one can dress decently with a body like that. The derriere! Sorry, love, I thought it was a pincushion."

And then there were the sessions with photographers barking orders to her that all but reduced her to tears—"Don't perspire, dollface," being one of the milder ones, and that one said under the heat of lights that would melt marble! She modeled a pink gray chiffon while descending from a carriage and pair in Rotten Row one chilly, misty morning, and, wrapped in yellow satin, she poured champagne on a barge in Chelsea Reach. Not to mention the hours she stood at Trafalgar Square while the photographer waited for just the right light to break through the clouds while just the right pigeon formation

29

scattered in front of where she stood on her protesting feet.

Morton, meanwhile, was late every day, huddled
with people from publicity, with Adela Cadoux, his
manager, or with bookkeeping. Even Benji was
going at a flat-out pace lately, with hardly enough
time for a change of clothes and a bite to eat. Even
that, though, was enough for Bliss to observe that
her brother had changed from the irresponsible he-
donist of a few weeks ago.

She saw him come in bushed, after a long day at
the shop, to hole up in the library after dinner with
Morton and old Mr. Ketchum, the head bookkeeper
—the only bookkeeper until Benji had joined the
firm. She wondered what was behind the pale, quiet
demeanor he displayed these days. Surely there was
nothing wrong with the MacHenry thing, or Morton
would have told her. Whatever it was, there were no
more late-night sessions at Schmidts listening to old
Elvis records, or marathon sessions at *Les Enfants
Terribles* with the Soho crowd that ended with
Benji's stumbling upstairs at daybreak, noisily singing off key.

Only Martha remained imperturbable. After a
particularly long session which included Morton,
Mr. Ketchum and Benji, they were airing the cigar
smoke from the draperies in the library when the
housekeeper said in her best doomsday voice, "I've
been with Henrys thirty-one years come spring
and I've seen their ups and I've seen their downs.
This Chez Henri thing"—she pronounced it *Shezz
Henry*—"might float the family; then again, it
might sink 'em to the bottom of the Thames. All
Mr. Morton has going for him is a knack for putting together a business that'll catch the public's

fancy. Before these frocks, it was turning old houses in Paddington into flats and then, once that was done, turning 'em back again. Hit 'em with a lick of paint and color the door some silly color and the same poor fools that sold 'em to him in the first place wants 'em back again."

"I didn't know that, Martha. That must have been before I came to London."

"It's the truth. He took what he made from that first business to buy this women's wear shop, and first thing you know, he'd done it again. Of course, he depends on folks like that snaky-eyed Reynaldo and all them seamstresses to do 'em up, and then it takes the likes of old Sam Ketchum and young Benji to tell him whether he's made a go of it."

Over dinner that night, Morton grew a bit nostalgic, thanks in part to the extra before-dinner drink he had taken to help him relax. The talk went from his boyhood summers to the later years when he had spent a few weeks off each year in the tiny, primitive cottage he still maintained in Yorkshire, and he wondered aloud if it was being kept up by the woman who was supposed to see to it for him.

"Lord knows when I'll have time to go again. The older I get, the shorter the years are—like the Doppler effect, they just seem to dash past and pile up behind me." He sighed.

While Morton continued to ramble on about putting his lovely herd of clotheshorses out to pasture and retiring to the wilds of Yorkshire, Bliss studied Benji. He was growing more and more morose these days, and she wondered if he was missing the Etchison girl. Lord knows, she wasn't missing the Etchison man! Whatever business he had

31

to conduct with Morton was evidently done at the shop, thank goodness, where her stint as a model for what the average American housewife would want when she had an evening on the town was ended. She missed her short-lived career as a model no more than she missed James Etchison. Just as she could do without snide remarks from the six-feet-tall mannequins who were all gaunt eyes, chiseled hips and collarbones, she could do without that searing, Arctic blast that made her feel like some street-corner dolly-bird.

"Bliss, come back from wherever you are," Morton called out playfully now. He had scarcely touched his beef tenderloin, she noticed, and she made a mental note to try to make him slow down a bit. For all their totally dissimilar interest, Bliss loved her cousin very much, and it suddenly occurred to her that he was looking every one of his years and then some. "I'm back, love," she answered lightly. "What did I miss?"

"I was saying that I'd like to give a small dinner party next weekend for, oh, half a dozen or so. We'll celebrate the winding up of all the red tape involved in getting one's feet wet in international commerce."

"Half a dozen. Hmmm." She mentally ran through what was involved in arranging something of this sort, with the dining-room chairs half redone and the man coming to do the ceiling. She decided that by putting in a series of twenty-hour days, she could just make it.

"I think I can handle it, although Sunday will suit better. Do I know them? Any food allergies or strong dislikes I should know about?"

"Oh, it will just be ourselves, the MacMurdles . . . three of them, by the way; the daughter's over for a visit. And then, of course, James and Leigh, Adela and . . . is Reade back yet?"

"Reade! Good Lord, I'd forgotten all about him," she exclaimed.

"Honestly, my dear, it looks as if you'd either marry the man or send him on his way," Morton told her with a rueful laugh. "You have no business keeping a fellow dangling that way, even if he is on the road half the time."

It was not Reade Johnston she was worried about; it was the Etchisons. The idea of entertaining them here at home brought a tightness to her midsection that not even the thought of Reade's return after a month in Portugal could allay.

That night as she snuggled down on her pale blue, lavender-scented sheets, she allowed her mind to come to grips with the problem of Reade. He had everything a woman could want in a man—looks, security, kindness. So why was it that, from the time he had left on a trip for his father's wine-importing business until he returned and called to take her out for dinner at one of the restaurants the firm did business with where the wine was usually better than the food, she never gave the man a thought?

Instead, she wasted time remembering the way another man's broad, angular back looked as he strode angrily away from her, or the way his slightly abrasive baritone voice raised goose bumps on her skin. How was it possible that a man she heartily disliked, not to mention distrusted, could make her more aware of her feminine vulnerability than any number of hours spent with the man she was, in all probability, going to marry someday? It just didn't make sense at all, she thought angrily, punching down her pillow as she tried to rid herself of the vision of his cool, disdainful eyes in his tanned, chiseled face.

The chairs were finished, their carefully selected tapestry blending well with the handsome draperies she had turned so that the sun-faded edges were not so evident. They probably should have been replaced, but they were so right for the lovely, small dining room with its dove-gray panels and white wainscoting that she had been forced to give into sentiment and had allowed them one more season. The ceiling had been restored to its former glory, and she and Martha had carefully washed and polished all two hundred and fifty prisms of the chandelier.

The menu was an easy one, cleverly chosen to appear more elaborate than it really was. Bliss herself had done most of the preparations before she went upstairs to change, leaving Martha with the last-minute touches and the instructions for the serving girl brought in for the occasion.

In her own room, Bliss bathed quickly and selected from among her fairly extensive wardrobe. Most of the clothes were chosen for her by Morton and reflected his taste more than her own more simple ideas. Usually she wore the things he gave her gladly, knowing he saw her an accessory of sorts to his position in the fashion industry. Tonight, however, she needed all the poise she could summon, and so she chose a dress she had bought in Ireland, a muted weave of gray, green and violet that looked for all the world like mist on a field of lavender. The styling was unobtrusive, the skirt delineating her nicely rounded hips and falling to the tips of her silver pumps. It was the neckline that gave her a momentary doubt; even the modest scoop was enough to reveal an expanse of creamy cleavage. She thought of the several times she had worn the dress before. She had not worried about modesty then, so what was so different about tonight?

As if she didn't know! Something about James Etchison, with his blatant, almost challenging masculinity, made her gauchely aware of her own femininity and she felt almost as if she should be buckling on a suit of armor. Defiantly, she sprayed on a generous whiff of Tearose perfume and twinkled wickedly as a fleeting thought struck her: What if James was allergic to roses?

Morton was waiting for her when she reached the bottom of the graceful, curving stairway, her hand trailing lightly on the polished baluster. "You look stunning, my dear," he greeted her.

He looked rather stunning himself, his black and white evening clothes pointing up his black and white hair dramatically—as he well knew. Bliss accepted his kiss and tucked her arm in his and they paused to view their images in the pier glass. Was Morton seeing an older version of Bliss beside him, the woman he had lost to his rather dashing cousin? Possibly. Was Bliss seeing a father image instead of the indulgent cousin who had given her a settled home for the first time in her life? Again—possibly.

The MacMurdles, Josh and Sybil, were as comfortable as old shoes, and Bliss, who had met them once or twice before, was soon sompletely at home with them. Their daughter, Rona, was another thing altogether. She had her father's tall, rangy build and her mother's pale beauty. Where on Sybil the years had softened her and an easygoing disposition had mellowed that beauty, on Rona it reached a high degree of polished perfection.

Bliss watched with more amusement than distaste as the young woman sized up and dismissed Benji and turned her considerable weapons on Morton. Adela had better look to her laurels tonight, for all her vaunted French chic might not be much good in the face of such young and predatory determination.

Reade brought flowers and Bliss thanked him and arranged the rather too perfect roses in a tall crystal vase. The slight tan he had acquired in Portugal was becoming to his regular features and sandy coloring, and Bliss waited for—almost *willed*—her pulses to acknowledge his return as she saw him settled with a drink and went to answer the door once more. She knew very well who it was and she took some time to brace herself and touch her hair in that instinctive gesture of female defensiveness.

She deliberately kept her eyes trained on Leigh as she opened the door and she didn't miss the swift, wary way the younger girl swept the room before she returned her glance to acknowledge her hostess.

"Good evening, Miss Bonner," came the gravelly baritone, and her eyes flew upward in spite of herself to take in the tall, angular man in a light twill trench coat.

"Good evening, Miss Etchison, Mr. Etchison. We're delighted you could make it tonight," she murmured, while her inner voice was screaming, Don't look at me that way! She had seen the quick narrowing of his heavy lids that covered a gleam of amusement and she knew as if he had spoken the words aloud that James Etchison was remembering the last time she had opened this door to him. She had been wearing a peach-colored silk robe then, pulled on hastily over a damp body. Now, as his eyes swiftly surveyed that same body in its sheer wool floor-length gown, she wished she had on a topcoat!

Dinner progressed peacefully enough and Bliss thanked her quick wits for thinking to ask Reade to be particularly nice to young Leigh. There had been a certain amount of tension when the men had stood to greet the new arrivals and Bliss had been unable to keep from looking from Leigh to Benji.

By the time they had finished the last course, Rona had shifted her attention from Morton to James, and Bliss watched with amusement, mixed with some other emotion she didn't care to identify, as the game of musical chairs progressed. Adela turned to capture Morton's attention and Benji, bless him, labored under a discussion of Labrador retrievers with Sybil MacMurdle and stole anguished glances at Leigh Etchison, while she, in turn, was bearing up under Reade's travelogue.

So the fire wasn't yet out under that particular kettle in spite of big brother's interference. Still, he must think he had the situation well in hand to risk bringing the two of them together tonight—unless he dared not go off and leave her alone.

As Morton fielded compliments on the dinner to Bliss and she accepted them with a murmured thanks, she was acutely aware of several speculative looks from James Etchison. Could it be that he was puzzled over her exact position in the Henry household? Or was she merely imagining those quizzical looks? All of these slightly unrealistic thoughts were wiped out of her mind when the men filed into Morton's study for an after-dinner cigar. James managed to cut Benji out of the flock for a quiet word and Bliss instinctively paused, allowing the other women to precede her into the drawing room while she watched apprehensively.

No more than half a minute passed while the two men stood in the hall talking, but it was enough. Benji's face took on an alarming pallor and she saw his lips tighten as he thrust out his chin in an expression of pure bravado.

James strolled on into the study and Bliss hurried to Benji's side. "What is it, Benji? Did he tear a strip off you for daring to look at his baby sister tonight? Blast that man! If he wants to keep her the ivory tower, he should never have brought her along!"

"Fat lot you know about anything," Benji muttered bitterly, removing his arm from her sympathetic hand.

Bliss stepped back in hurt surprise. It was not like Benji to be surly, in spite of his sometimes brash behavior. Could it be that his strained looks were due to something more serious than just being denied the pleasure of Leigh's company? But then, perhaps he truly loved the girl.

Turning away to rejoin the women, Bliss tightened her lips in determination; if that was the case, then she would delight in doing everything in her power to see that the two of them had a chance; the Devil take James Etchison and his eighteenth-century tactics!

Reade was waiting to waylay her as she walked through the double doors. "Come out into the garden with me for a minute, Bliss. I haven't had a minute alone with you in a month!"

"Oh, Reade, I can't. After all, I am hostess and it—"

He interrupted her impatiently. "From the looks

of things, no one will even notice we're missing. That brother of yours is mooning around over the Etchison kid, and the MacMurdles are talking shop with Morton and Adela. As for the gold-plated Rona, she's got her hooks well into the tall, grim type and he's lapping it up wholesale! Come on . . . here, I'll get you a wrap."

There was nothing for it but to accompany him into the floodlighted garden. If she knew Reade, he would head for the shadowy areas and try to make up for lost time. Funny—she liked him as well as any man she knew, barring Morton and Benji of course, but his kisses left her cold. Maybe there was something lacking in her.

"You look exquisite tonight," he whispered as he put her cape around her shoulders. "I like that dress . . . it's in perfect taste."

Just for a fleeting, wicked moment, she wished she had worn one of the more outrageous gowns she possessed. "Thank you, Reade," she said politely, allowing him to usher her through the French doors and out onto the loggia.

Once beyond the reach of the hidden outdoor lights, Reade wasted no time in turning her to him and pulling her close. Bliss pulled stiffly away, not wanting to hear what she saw he was determined to say. But when he leaned down to kiss her, she didn't resist, all the while wondering how she had allowed things to drift on to this extent.

"I'm sorry, Reade," she said miserably when he lifted his lips from hers. "I don't seem to be very good company tonight."

"You're tired, of course, my darling. If I know you, you've allowed yourself to be run ragged getting this thing together for Morton. He uses you shamefully, but it doesn't have to go on, you know."

"I've enjoyed every minute of preparing for tonight," she argued. "Morton doesn't exploit his friends, Reade. He's the kindest, most generous man I've ever known, and I'd do anything to repay him for taking us in and giving us a home all these years. He's been the making of Benji, providing him with a good job when he left school. He was disappointed that I didn't want to get involved with the business, but he allowed me to putter around here just because it makes me happy."

"All right, all right, I take it back. But all the same, Bliss, it can't go on indefinitely. That Cadoux woman will land him one of these days and then you'll be out in the cold."

Bliss braced herself, knowing what was coming. She didn't want to have to deal with it, didn't want to think of a time when her life would change from its pleasant, comfortable routine.

"I'll be taking over the home office for Dad anytime I want to. All these trips have left me pretty well *au fait* as far as the suppliers are concerned and so I could settle down now. We might even start to redecorate a flat of our own. Dad says there's plenty of space at home and Mother would lend a hand."

It was all Bliss could do not to shudder. The Johnstons were very kind and they doted on their only child, but all the same, how could she even consider living in their home, subject to their likes and dislikes, their tastes and misdirected generosity? Reade did not know her at all if he thought she could be happy under those circumstances. Yet a small, chilling fear took root in her mind.

What if things *did* change here? What if Morton *did* marry? He was certainly a very eligible man still, and Adela was frank in her cool, almost uninterested pursuit. One thing was certain: If Adela came to Morton's home as his wife, there would no longer be room here for Bliss. And she was not at all certain she could manage on her own, never having tried.

While Reade waited, nuzzling her hair in a way that vaguely irritated her, Bliss pondered these and other uncomfortable ideas. Reade said he loved her; perhaps she could learn to love him as well. Or perhaps she already did; how could she tell? She had nothing to which to compare the relationship.

The intrusive sound of a deep, rough voice made her start almost guiltily and pull away from Reade's arms as she turned to face James Etchison.

"I don't mean to intrude," he said urbanely, "but I thought perhaps the dark blue Renault with the leaking tire might be yours, Johnston."

"Well, blast!" Reade exploded. "That's a brandnew set of radials that set me back plenty, I can tell you!" The rest of his muttering was lost as they watched him disappear at a trot around the corner of the house, and then Bliss made as if to go inside.

"Just a moment, if you don't mind, Miss Bonner," James said, turning to take her arm.

She pulled away. "But I do mind, Mr. Etchison. I'm a little chilly and I think I'd better go back in to my guests." Her voice was as haughty as she could make it, considering the unfortunate effect the man always seemed to have on her.

"Don't worry about your guests, Miss Bonner; they can manage for another few minutes without your gracious presence. And if it was something else you were worried about, then let me put your mind at rest. You're in no danger from me. I'll leave the sampling of your delightful kisses to men who don't mind queueing up for them."

She stiffened as if he had struck her, head thrown back and eyes sparkling dangerously. Her voice, when she spoke, was trembling with anger. "We have absolutely nothing to say to each other, Mr. Etchison, and now I'm going inside and you can go straight to . . ."

"Thank you, Miss Bonner; you've made your opinion of me perfectly clear from the first time we had the misfortune to meet. May I just reassure you that the feeling is mutual. However, this has nothing to do with you in a personal sense. It's your brother who concerns me, and if you care at all for him, you'll take time to hear what I have to say."

Without waiting for her to reply, he ushered her ungently to the aged stone bench beside the ornamental fishpond and sat her down, taking his place beside her before she could jump up again. The light from a French window filtered through the glossy viburnums and she could feel his glance strike her face as she schooled herself not to respond to his disturbing nearness. "What about Benji?" she managed to say with a surprisingly steady, if somewhat husky, voice.

"Just this, Miss Bonner: I've spoken to Leigh and to your brother more than once and I sent her away to get her out of his range. Unfortunately, the friends she was staying with had a family emergency and she came back. But you're going to make it clear to that young wastrel, just as I've made it clear to Leigh, that they are *not* to see each other alone. He is *not* to call, *not* to try to get her to meet him; and if there's any more bother on that score, I'll see that he gets more trouble than he ever bargained for. Your brother, Miss Bonner, might have a good-looking face and a plausible sort of charm that impresses schoolgirls, but he has no character and no integrity, and I won't have my sister wasting herself on a chap who will probably end up doing time!"

She was stunned. Absolutely shattered! Whatever she had expected, it had not been this cold, calculated attack on her brother as a person. "Is . . . is that quite all, Mr. Etchison?" she made herself reply.

He stood up, his lean, rugged frame under the flawless evening clothes somehow threatening. Bliss also got to her feet hurriedly, unsteadily, only to find herself far too close to him. She stepped back and her knee struck the edge of the bench, and when she caught her breath, he put out a hand to steady her.

His voice was as impersonal as his touch. "That's all."

"Just a minute," she blurted out breathlessly when he moved away from her. "You implied that there was something more than just the fact that you want to keep them apart. Exactly what are you accusing my brother of, Mr. Etchison? May I know that?"

"No, you may not, Miss Bonner." He raked her with a glance that left her even more shaken, seeming to take her apart and examine each aspect of her curiously, much as one would study some strange, unknown specimen.

"But you can't just—"

"Suffice it to say that your brother knows that I'm onto him now and that there'll be no more trouble on that front or the roof will fall in on him. As far as

43

my sister is concerned, it's unavoidable that they'll be meeting occasionally, since we're more or less compelled to maintain some sort of front. But that's the extent of it. I refuse to allow my own social pattern to be changed just to accommodate a pair of reckless children. So you will impress on young Benjamin that he's not to attempt to take advantage of the circumstances. Is that clear?"

She swallowed painfully, indignant for her brother and, what was infinitely worse, crushed to know the extent of this man's contempt for herself. "Quite clear," she answered faintly.

"Good. And now, if you'll excuse me, I've promised Miss MacMurdle a tour of some of our better nightspots. A very beautiful woman, Miss MacMurdle, don't you think?" They were strolling back along the graveled paths as calmly as if they had been discussing the possibilities for next year's Chelsea show.

"Very," Bliss agreed weakly.

"And refreshingly honest," he continued in an irritatingly conversational tone.

Honest! Rona MacMurdle? A pit viper was honest, too, but that didn't make it any more acceptable!

Chapter Three

Bliss stared distractedly at the full, loose arrangement on the hall table for several minutes. Then she turned away, leaving the tiny, waxy-pink viburnum blossoms in untidy drifts across the polished surface. Apathetically, she moved into the morning room and dropped down onto a muted chintz-covered ottoman. She was worried about Benji, yet the one time she had approached him and tried to bring up the subject of Leigh Etchison, he had snapped her head off.

"I'm sorry, Bliss . . . truly," he had apologized immediately afterward. "I think I must be needing a vacation."

"I've been thinking you might need a tonic," Bliss retorted.

Morton, joining them at that moment, suggested that Benji might like to take a few days off and drive up to the cottage in Yorkshire. "It's a good place to walk off some of what's ailing you, I always found, and you'd be doing me a favor. I haven't looked in to see that everything's all right in far too long."

At first Benji had seemed hesitant, but in the end he seemed to look forward to getting off into the wilds alone. After he left, the atmosphere was a good bit lighter, although Morton was too deeply involved in going over plans for the advertising theme for MacHenry, Inc., to be much company. When Bliss chided him for working too hard, he told her with unusual asperity that his own future, plus a good amount of James Etchison's money, rode on the success of the venture, a fact that caused her more than a little uneasy speculation.

Etchison Limited was a holding company which put its considerable resources behind firms seeking to expand after considering very carefully whether or not it would be a sound investment. It was a source of great pride to Morton that his own small business was considered to be worthy of larger backing, and he spoke often and glowingly of the man who was coming to haunt the outer fringes of Bliss's mind in spite of all she could do.

On the Saturday night after Benji had left for Yorkshire, both Bliss and Morton agreed that a night on the town would do them a world of good— blow away the cobwebs, so to speak. Morton urged her to wear one of Reynaldo's creations that had been altered to fit her. With a certain feeling of rebellion, she selected the most daring of all—a slashed halter of bronze georgette over acres of swirling skirts. Her skirt was covered with scintillating gold sequins. The look suggested rather more than was actually revealed.

Reade, whom she had put off the last two times he had called, would be scandalized. But it was not Reade of whom she thought when she took a last appraising look in her cheval glass. There were new hollows under her cheekbones, and despite the daring cut of the halter, the swell of her rounded young breasts was less noticable than usual. She had lost weight for some reason and she decided with a certain amount of satisfaction that it became her.

The dinner was a great success and Bliss made a point of analyzing and remembering the unusual amandine sauce for the trout. It was not until the lights were dimming for the cabaret that she spotted James. With him, to her dismay, was Rona MacMurdle, looking devastating as only a black-clad blonde can.

After a show in which she neither saw nor heard anything, Bliss was more than ready to go home. But as luck would have it, they were spotted by a business acquaintance of Morton's who insisted on buying them one more drink. Unfortunately, he had already had more than the traffic would bear, and when he asked Bliss to dance while Morton settled with the waiter for their dinner, she obliged simply because she didn't want a scene. Knowing Bruce Pittmann from a few past occasions, she knew he was all too capable of becoming ugly at a moment's notice.

The band was good and any other time, with any other partner, Bliss could have enjoyed it. As it was, she was having a hard time keeping Bruce's hand from dropping down to her hips as he nuzzled her ear, holding her unnecessarily close. When she begged him to give her room to breathe, he danced her close to the veranda doors. Before she could prevent him, he had steered her into a glassed-in, unused room, empty in winter except for bare tables and a rack of folding chairs along some potted plants.

"Please, Bruce, I'd prefer to return to Morton," Bliss insisted firmly. She made an attempt to edge her way around the table and back to the doors, but he waylaid her with gay alcoholic cunning.

"Ah-ah, little lady, not until you give ol' uncle Brucie a li'l kiss. Gotta kiss Miss Bliss," he taunted, lurching toward her as she sidestepped once more.

Where was Morton? she thought as she panicked, trying to overcome her disgust. In a decent place like this it was unthinkable that she should be subjected to such behavior! Just because Bruce Pittmann happened to be in a position to parade his mistresses at Chez Henri and dress them from the top of Morton's line was no reason why he could be allowed to offend the supper club's customers—although she had to admit in all honesty that Bruce was probably a far better customer than she would ever be.

"Stop it, Bruce! You have no right to make me stay out here! Now leave me alone or I'll scream and let the management take care of you!" Cornered between two droopy palms and a chair rack, she crossed her arms defensively and glared at him. When she saw his feral eyes grow brighter, she should have been prepared.

He caught her, his damp, heavy hands on her shoulder, and her struggles only seemed to incite him. Her head was twisted away to avoid his mouth, and the fumes of alcohol on his breath sickened her. She kicked out and missed. As she kicked again, she felt his arms drop from her shoulders, and then she was standing shakily on her feet.

"Are you all right?" James asked.

Bliss blinked from him to the now pathetic-looking man who had almost overpowered her a second ago and nodded as Bruce lurched away, looking flushed and slightly untidy but not at all repentant.

"Don't think about him," James told her as he followed the direction of her gaze. "He should have been sent home hours ago, but he's a member, so the management tends to be lenient. You'd do better to learn to say no and mean it."

"I . . ." She shrugged helplessly. What could she say? "I didn't want to make a scene," she offered lamely.

His eyes narrowed on her, skimming the contours of her body in the revealing dress, and his expression was contemptuous when he nodded toward the slashed neckline. "I think the legal term is an attractive nuisance, meaning the owner is at fault for issuing a tacit invitation."

Bliss's nerves were ragged. She was tired, and besides, something about this man always made her overreact. Impulsively, she swung at him and her palm made a clear, strangely satisfying sound as it connected with his cheek.

For perhaps a full minute they stared at each other, Bliss aghast at what she had done, no matter what the provocation. James's withering gaze chilled her like a blast from the Arctic. Then he reached for her, and this time there was no escape, no rescue. He brought his mouth down on hers and she was as helpless before that force as a mesmerized rabbit.

Almost before she realized what was happening he had put her away from him, a scathing look of contempt on his face as he took in her bone-white face, her brimming, frightened eyes and the bruised, trembling mouth. For just an instant, something shifted in his disparaging eyes, a fleeting look of puzzlement that was gone so quickly that Bliss thought afterward she must have imagined it.

He left her then, disappearing as abruptly as he had come. After she had composed herself as much as possible, Bliss made her way back to the table, where Morton was engaged in conversation with a friend. He looked up and stood when she approached, asking if she was all right.

"I saw you dancing with Bruce Pittmann and was on my way to the rescue when Edward here caught me. I'm afraid we were busy catching up on the news and time slipped away. Bruce didn't step out of line, did he?"

"Nothing I couldn't take care of," Bliss told him, struggling to eradicate the memory of another set of arms.

The scent of his aftershave was still in her nostrils. The taste of him was still on her lips long after she went to bed that night. In desperation, she began naming the plants in her garden, beginning with abelia and finally falling asleep somewhere around mignonette.

A week later, Morton was called on to make a quick trip to the States. "I think I'm beginning to find out something about myself," he quipped as Bliss carefully folded his shirts and placed them in the pigskin two-suiter. "I'm not cut out for playing the part of an international business tycoon. One small, moderately successful dress shop with a line of original designs was more my speed."

Bliss reassured him, all the while wondering if he weren't right. Now that the deal was made, Morton seemed to be losing momentum. The fun was in the hunt, not the kill.

She drove him to the airport and he promised to call within a day or so and let her know how long he would be gone. "Look after your brother, Bliss. I wish to goodness he had more of your sweet stability, but I'm afraid he takes more after your father. Drew was always a bit of an adventurer . . . only in the nicest sense of the word, you understand," he hurried to add, and Bliss nodded that she understood. Her father *had* been an adventurer, a larger-than-life character who was only beginning to show signs of settling down when he and his wife went down somewhere in the South Atlantic during an ill-fated sailing race.

Keeping her promise to Morton proved more difficult than she had anticipated. Benji was out late each night, often not coming home for dinner. When Bliss tried to question him, he passed her off with one lame excuse or another, and she knew he was lying. What was worse, he knew she knew he was lying, and that hurt. In the past they had always been truthful to each other, with Benji avoiding an answer rather than giving a direct lie.

There was a look of strain about him, too, and that worried her even more. She recalled all too vividly what James Etchison had said about his calling trouble down on his own head. But she seemed unable to reach him these days, watching helplessly as he went about with an almost desperate sort of gaiety.

There had been several mentions in the gossip columns of James and the American beauty he was being seen about town with, but none of Leigh. Bliss assumed the younger girl had returned to her friends in Cornwall. She wondered when Rona MacMurdle was going back home or *if* she was going back home. She seemed to have made an instant hit with James, and if he preferred his women sophisticated, shallow and more than a little hedonistic, then more power to him. They deserved each other!

Morton called to say that he would be in New York the better part of a week and that she was not to wear herself out trying to do all the redecorating of the house again. He knew her penchant for trying to accomplish the more unsettling tasks when he was away, but she made no promises. She loved working in the handsome old home. She was amply rewarded for every hour of labor by the many more hours of pleasure she found in simply basking in the atmosphere created by the gleaming old furniture, its slightly faded elegance scented with beeswax and lemon oil, and flowers she had nurtured.

Two days after Morton called, Benji told her he was going away for the weekend and asked if she could lend him some money.

"Darling, what on earth have you done with all yours? Don't tell me you've taken up following the horses!" She laughed, mentally juggling her budget so as to allow him the lion's share. She knew she shouldn't, since Benji had more than she did with the annuity they shared and his salary. But then it must be expensive dating on a more or less regular basis. If Reade spent half as much on her as Benji seemed to on his girls, she would have a guilt complex a mile high! On the one or two nights a week she saw Reade, they usually dined at a moderately priced restaurant, went to a cinema or simply stayed home and munched as they watched the telly.

By the time Benji clattered downstairs with a bag in his hand and his heavy coat over his shoulders, she had the envelope ready. He peered inside, tucked it away inside his jacket and kissed the side of her nose. "Thanks, love. Knew I could count on you," he said, not quite meeting her eyes. "Look for me when you see me. Old Ketchum said he'd hold the fort until I got back."

As he dashed out the front door Bliss hurried after him. "Wait! Benji, where will you be? How can I reach you if anything comes up?"

"Nothing will. It never does," he called back airily, vaulting into his red sports car. Who but Benji would put the top down in the middle of winter?

Both hands in the pockets of her tan flannel skirt, she wondered why she wasted her time worrying about him. Benji would soon be twenty-five, after all. She had her own life to sort out. Lately she had been thinking more and more about changes. Just what sorts of changes she was hard put to say. But sometimes she caught herself almost listening for something, some sign. She shivered as a colder gust than usual blew a flurry of beech leaves across the crocus bed.

Perhaps she was like the crocus bulbs, sleeping confidently in the knowledge that there would be an awakening of some sort, whether it be to sunshine, to snow or to mist and rain. Was it some sixth sense, a sort of biological clock that had already begun the unwinding mechanism that led inevitably to the sounding of a new hour?

She dismissed such foolish meanderings and busied herself with polishing the collection of porcelain that was Morton's pride and joy. When Martha came into the drawing room to announce her plans to visit her sister for the evening, Bliss told her not to be in a hurry to come back. "There's only me, and I'll probably take a sandwich up and have an early night with a book. Take a break while you can, Martha, and give my love to the children."

True to her word, she took a tray upstairs, but instead of eating, she pottered about her room, opening and closing drawers distractedly. She had just begun to change into her robe when the front-door bell sounded and she hastily slipped her arms back into the ivory silk blouse and skirt. She could think of no one who might be calling at this hour unless Martha had returned early, but then she would have let herself in.

All of this speculation brought her to the door and she opened it to see James Etchison, looking seven feet tall in his anger.

"Déjà vu," Bliss observed flippantly, trying to keep herself from flying into a million shattered pieces.

"All right, where is he?" James demanded, brushing her aside to step into the foyer. His freezing hot eyes burned through her and she felt utterly defenseless, despite the fact that this time, at least, she was completely dressed. "He did come home last night, I presume. What I want to know is, where is he now? Speak to me!

"You haven't given me a chance to speak to you!" she retorted. She was managing to maintain a creditable degree of poise even if her pulse was hammering at her temples. "Where is who? Morton?"

"Your brother, that's who, as if you didn't know!

Don't tell me you weren't in on it! No sooner does Leigh get back from the country than that scoundrel starts hanging around again, and now she's taken off and I want to know just where she is!"

"Look, if you want me to tell you anything, you're going to have to simmer down and start from the beginning," Bliss declared, leading the way into the morning room, where the remnants of a fire still glowed on the hearth. "I don't have the slightest idea what you're raving on about, but if you've mislaid your sister, then I can assure you you won't find her here."

"You think this is some kind of joke?" he barked. "You'll find very little to laugh about before I'm through, I can assure *you!*"

Bliss sat down because, in spite of the iron control she was exercising over her temper, her knees were showing signs of falling down on the job. James pulled out a cigarette and gripped it between his lips, lighting it with a sharp flick of a small gold lighter. He continued to pace restlessly, blowing streams of smoke through his flaring nostrils, and then he began to talk. "She stayed in her room all day, said she had a headache. She's been quiet lately . . . too quiet; and I suppose I was a fool not to have suspected something, but I didn't! At any rate, when I got home from the office, she was not in her room. Not only that, her purse was gone, and her coat and at least some of her clothes. She told no one where she was going and nobody saw her leave, so I can only assume she didn't want any questions asked."

"But why do you think Benji might have been involved? She could have—"

"He's the only one I've forbidden her to see. If she were with anyone else, then there would be no need to be so secretive about it. So where is he?" He turned on her, his feet braced aggressively on the faded Bessarabian carpet.

"I don't know! All I know is that he said he was going off for the weekend, but I don't know where . . . honestly, James, that's the truth." Her mind was frantically sorting through the details of Benji's departure, searching for some clue she might have overlooked. She shook her head in bewilderment. "Look, all I know is that he left just after lunch and said he might be longer than just the weekend. If you'll just leave me alone, I may be able to come up with something . . . but I can't promise."

She raised her eyes to plead for time, for space in which to think. The tall, rangy build of the man before her, as large as it was, wasn't sufficient to contain the seething, ruthless energy he generated. Bliss felt as if she were being swept away by a tidal wave. "Half a day?" she begged.

"Half the night, you mean? It's almost ten now! How long do you think I can stand it?"

Bliss jumped to her feet, too agitated to sit still under the burning accusation in his eyes. There was an anguish there that cut her to the quick, in spite of her dislike of the man and his bullying tactics. The girl was his sister, after all, and she was little more than a child. "Look, if you'll just go home and let me think, I promise you I'll come up with something! He can't have gone without leaving some clue." She was stretching the truth and she knew it. So, she suspected, did James. But what else could the man do?

His shoulders slumped, and she checked an impulse to reach out her hand to brush the hair from his forehead. It was the first time she had seen him

looking anything but perfectly groomed in his flawlessly tailored Bond Street clothes, and it somehow
made him seem touchingly human, vulnerable.

Somewhere deep inside her, some vestige of self-
preservation warned her against allowing herself to
be fooled by this man. He was as cold and heartless
as a marble statue where anyone except his sister was
concerned. And perhaps Rona MacMurdle, although she found it hard to believe he could show
the same depth of concern for the beautiful American as he did for Leigh.

Half an hour later she left Benji's room, her mind
still working to fit together several parts of a puzzle.
He had taken some of his oldest clothes, as well as
his new dark green suede pants and the matching
vest. Something clicked in her mind and she hurried
to the kitchen, opening the cabinet door where
Martha kept the several keys to various doors and
storage units. One key was conspicuous by its
absence—the key to Morton's cottage in Yorkshire.

Within half an hour she was on her way. She had
taken a map and a flashlight and had located Morton's spare key on an old ring he kept in his stud box.
There had been no time to call James, and besides,
she wanted to reach them first. No telling what
James might do in his present mood if he came to the
isolated cottage with its one bedroom and found
the pair of them together. Mayhem was not outside
the realm of possibility, and under the circumstances
he might be justified.

It was pitch dark, with a cold, wet wind groaning
around her little Mini, when Bliss turned off onto the
narrow, rugged country road and continued driving
for about a mile and a half. She had forgotten just

how rough the country was, now very dark, miles and miles from the nearest village—and that was little more than a few farms and a pub. There had evidently been some heavy rains in the past that had eroded the trail until it was all but impassable in spots. Probably, if she had made the trip in the daylight, she would never have dared bring her car up this far. But the idea of tackling the trail on foot was unthinkable at this time of night. She could very well wander off and die of exposure before anyone found her.

The cottage looked less than inviting, its two tiny windows all battened down with shutters that had long since lost any vestige of paint. There was no sign of a light and she didn't smell smoke on the damp air. Could she have been so wrong, then? Why would Benji have taken the key if he had no intention of coming here? And he had taken it, she knew, because he had returned it after that weekend when he had come up here alone to check on the place for Morton.

Her heart sank as she pushed open the heavy door and smelled the mustiness. Surely no one had been in here for weeks, at least. There was a faint, pungent odor of ashes, but that would have been from Benji's last trip. It would never have occurred to him to clean out the fireplace and lay a fire for the next comer.

With her torch she located two candles and a lamp with a sooty chimney. She lighted the lamp and took stock of her surroundings. There was not much to see, really. One room up, one down, and both just large enough to take a deep breath in. Up in the loft, a double bed took up almost all the floorspace. At least the bed had been made up, although she found no blankets except for one eiderdown. Downstairs, there was the main room, which held two chairs, a small table and a fireplace, plus a bookshelf. Other than that, there was the lean-to kitchen and a bath of sorts, with only a curtain separating the two. There was a camp stove and a pitcher pump over a soapstone sink, and from there the facilities deteriorated.

One blessing—there was a well-stocked pantry at one end of the kitchen. It was only a few boards put up crudely, but every shelf was filled with tinned food and there were two jars of instant coffee. At least she wouldn't starve before she could get out of here.

But for now, sleep was highest on her priority list. She was totally exhausted and, in spite of the fact that she had not had any dinner, she was too far gone to eat. Tomorrow she would try to come up with some alternative solution, and when she did . . . *if* she did . . . then and only then would she call James Etchison. Meanwhile, she was safe from his harassment, tucked into a damp bed that was soft and warming up nicely under the light comfort of the eiderdown.

Sometime during the night she aroused to hear the wonderfully soothing sound of rain on the steeply sloping roof. There was another sound, but it was not enough to awaken her; she only stirred and turned over, murmuring something unintelligible before she lapsed back into the deep sleep of total exhaustion.

Chapter Four

Bliss opened her eyes slowly and stared at the tiny window that looked out into the bare treetops. Yesterday's high, light cloud cover had descended and now it blocked out all but the thinnest light, seeming to hover and sag like a bundle of dirty laundry. Blinking to clear her vision, she seemed to recall the soporific sound of rain on the roof. But there was no such sound now, only an intermittent scratch as fitful gusts of wind blew a branch against the side of the house. An occasional disconsolate drip sounded from somewhere outside, but there was another sound, a much more subtle one that she could not identify.

Lying there on her side, with one small foot peeping from under the eiderdown as she dangled it over the edge of the bed, Bliss forced herself to comg to grips with her problems. Benji was gone and she hadn't the slightest idea where he was, and Leigh

Etchison was gone, as well. Odds were they were together, and it was up to Bliss to locate the pair of them before James did—if she valued her brother's neck.

The cottage was cold as only a rock house can be, but there was a basket of kindling on the hearth and logs in the box. Would it be worth building a small fire before she left just to get dressed beside its warmth? She could make herself a breakfast of sorts before she hit the road. . . .

The road! That drip—and the clouds! Good Lord, what sort of idiot was she, lying here dreaming while the road down the hill became impassable.

Throwing back the eiderdown, she sat up and leaned back on her hand to brace herself while she fumbled about on the icy floor for her shoes. She had slept in tights and a sweater last night, rather an unorthodox outfit, but not at all uncomfortable. She hooked her toes into one shoe, and when it threatened to fall off, she leaned back on her elbow and raised her foot in the air. Then the bed shifted.

"Mmmmm, ahhhhh. What's going on, hmmm?" came a deep, drowsy voice so close behind her that her skin actually shifted on her spine.

Bliss drew back her hand as if she had stuck it into a fire. When she jumped off the bed, the eiderdown came with her, revealing to her stunned eyes the recumbent form of James Etchison. Somewhere, in some primitive memory bank, she must have stored up the details of that sight—the long, powerful legs with their covering of short, dark hair, the briefs and T-shirt that emphasized the masculinity of the wearer, the dark hair with its light sprinkling of silver falling thickly over his creased forehead. His eyes were open and he was staring at her with none of the stunned amazement that she herself was feeling. While her mind was groping for a hold on reality, she was registering the irrelevant fact that with his hair all untidy and a dark shadow on that formidable jaw, James Etchison looked more human than she thought possible, which, under the circumstances, was an utterly disconcerting idea.

"What are you doing in my bed?" she demanded fiercely, clutching the covers around her body as she stood shivering on the freezing floor.

"I was sleeping until someone put a hand on my stomach and leaned on it," came a dry reply.

"Get out of here this minute! You have . . . I've never . . . !" she sputtered impotently, her eyes more frightened than she knew in her sleep-flushed face.

"Calm down a minute, Bliss," he said tiredly, swinging his legs over the side in an easy motion.

She backed away and found herself smack up against the damp, cold plaster wall. The room was hardly large enough for the bed, never mind the people. "You have three minutes to get your clothes on and get out of here. If you're not gone by the time I get back from . . . get back, I'll—"

"You'll call the police, right? And after that, would you mind calling room service and having them send up a pot of coffee and a menu? Oh, and signal me when you're through. I could do with a shave." He rubbed a tanned, well-shaped hand over his stubble, and Bliss stood frozen as she slowly absorbed the meaning of his words.

There was no phone. There were no near neighbors, and even if there were, after last night's rain there would be no going or coming until at least half a day's sunshine had dried the mud. The very isolation that had appealed to Morton and had ensured his privacy now threatened to maroon her here with the last man on earth she would have chosen to be imprisoned with.

And from the looks of it, he felt exactly the same way about her. "Well," he prompted in a surly tone, "shall I go first? I think we've passed the stage of unctuous politeness."

Wrapping the comforter more securely around her, Bliss gathered up the things she had worn the day before and scrambled with more haste than dignity from the room and down the ladder. She shut herself up in the freezing makeshift bath and made what ablutions she could using Morton's toothbrush and a sliver of shaving soap. When she came out, she felt as if she were now more able to cope with her uninvited guest.

The aroma of freshly made coffee prompted an uneasy truce, and they sat, one on either side of the small fire James had made, and sipped the reviving liquid. From time to time Bliss was aware of his speculative glance, but she was not ready to jump into the fray just yet. So she took care to avoid those cool, appraising eyes. He obviously suspected her of spiriting away the two miscreants, and so far she hadn't a theory at all to explain what could have happened to them, not a clue!

She could have sworn they had come here. That weekend Benji had come alone would have been fresh in his mind, and when he wanted a place to be alone with his girl, what better plan than to slip away up here in the wilds of Yorkshire? The key was missing, too, which made it even more puzzling. . . .

"James!" In her distress, she was not even aware of having called him by his first name. "What if something has happened to them? I mean a road accident! In the darkness . . . the rain . . ."

"You forget, it wasn't raining when they left, nor was it dark. There'd have been reports and one of us would have been notified."

Her shoulders settled dispiritedly as she turned her empty eyes to the small blaze that was rapidly dispelling the dampness in the cramped but cozy room.

He spoke again. "What made you so certain they had come this way? When I called, Martha had just gotten in and she hadn't found your note yet. She was worried and called me back when she did. But even so, we both thought you were only guessing."

Bliss explained about the key and the clothes Benji had taken, which were the same ones he had worn up here the first time he had come, except for the new suede outfit. "His hiking boots were missing from his closet, and I just didn't know where else to begin," she explained. "The key . . . he had returned it after his last trip, and then the clothes . . . it all seemed to add up, but now I don't know what to believe." She allowed her eyes to stray to the cold, gray scene outside, where a misting rain was beginning to obscure the wooded hills.

"I don't know what sort of things Leigh packed. It didn't occur to me to check up, but then, I suppose a woman's mind works differently from a man's," James observed.

Bliss couldn't decide whether she was being insulted in some subtle way or not. So, after one swift, doubtful glance, she looked away, deep in her own troubled thoughts, in which James Etchison figured least.

By noon, the rain was even heavier, coming down

as if it had no beginning and no end, and Bliss reluctantly abandoned any hope of making it back down the hill before nightfall. They might be stuck here for days at this rate, and Bliss was already beginning to feel as if she were caged up with a tiger. James had smoked almost a full pack of cigarettes, had drunk two pots of coffee and had not eaten a bite. His hair was looking even more untidy than when she had first laid eyes on him that morning. His beard was casting a shadow over his face once again, and she thought he must be one of those men who shaved twice a day, which, for no logical reason, made her even more apprehensive.

"Oh, God!" he cried, smacking a fist into the palm of his hand as he stood up, his shoulders stiff under the dark, coarse knit sweater. "What am I doing here when they could be anywhere? I've looked after that child since she was ten, and now . . ." He broke off with a string of profanity that made Bliss's color deepen.

She was laying the table for an evening meal, not that she expected James to eat anything. But she had to do something and there was scant scope for her nervous energy in that tiny, primitive cottage.

If she had waited for him to apologize for his outburst, she would have been disappointed. For all he knew, she didn't exist once he had pumped her dry of information. He ignored her completely.

Which was a relief, really. He might have been distinctly vindictive to her instead of being merely unpleasant. He had held her somehow responsible for her brother's actions in the beginning. Now, however, he seemed only concerned for his sister's well-being, and that was reassuring. A man who cared so deeply for his sister would understand her own concern for her brother—that is, if he stopped to consider the affair from her point of view. If there had been an accident of any sort, then she was just as vulnerable as he was.

By dinnertime the rain, which had stopped for a little over an hour to allow a thin, yellowish sun to smile wanly on them, had started again in earnest. Bliss's tattered nerves were wearing thin. James was a pacer and there was simply no room to pace. Even though she sat huddled up in one of the two chairs, trying to make herself small, the vibrations of two worried, agitated adults in the cramped space was too much. It was as if the energy he emitted so furiously ricocheted from the hard walls to bombard her. When, without even glancing at her, he refused the meal she had prepared from tins, she blew up.

"Why don't you just leave! Get out of here! Go sit in your car or prowl through the woods or . . . or slide down a mountain, but just get out! I can't *stand* being cooped up in here with you another minute! I hate you! I hate this place and I hate . . ." The words were strangled in her throat as sobs overcame her and she turned her face to the wall and wept noisily, painfully, not with the quiet release of ladylike tears. There was too much inside her that stormed for escape, too many hours of worry over Benji, too much tension that had been building from the moment she had awakened and found that she was not alone.

The hand that fell upon her shaking shoulders was firm as it turned her away from the wall, but gentle nonetheless. Bliss was beyond protest and could only follow the line of least resistance. She leaned against the hard, warm strength James offered, accepting the comforting arms that enclosed

her, the softly murmured words that had no meaning
beyond their soothing tone. When a large handkerchief, slightly wrinkled but crisp and fresh-smelling,
was pushed into her hand, she made good use of it.
Only when her breath had become steadier between
the gulps and compulsive little gasps that caught in
her throat did she lean away to look searchingly up
into his dark, grimly shadowed face.

"Better now?" he asked.

Wordlessly, she nodded, needing space in which
to pull herself together but dreading moving away
from the unlikely haven. When at last he stepped
back, still retaining a light grip on her arm, the air
seemed unduly cold on her body in spite of the
cashmere sweater. But she braced herself and smiled
tremulously at him.

"I think we'd better have that meal you promised.
It occurs to me that it's been hours since I last ate,
and I expect we could both think better with something in our stomachs."

The soup needed reheating, but they finished what
she had prepared and then James made another pot
of coffee.

"All right, now, let's take stock of where we are
and where we're going," he said, leaning back in his
chair to dig out his lighter. Bliss was uncomfortably
aware of what a sight she must be after her outburst,
especially as she had slept in her sweater and her suit
was none too fresh after yesterday's drive.

"Hell," James muttered, flicking the small gold
lighter to no avail. He stood up and glanced around,
his eyes coming to rest on the brass box on the
mantel where the matches were kept. As he reached
for it he hesitated, then picked up a folded piece of
paper beside it. As he looked at it, Bliss, who had

watched him absently as her mind tangled with the problems at hand, saw the color drain from his face.

"What is it?"

Wordlessly, he handed it over, dropping down into his chair with his head coming to rest heavily in his hands. "God!" he exclaimed, a world of feeling in that one word.

The note was short and to the point:

Bliss,
Sorry about this, but we had no choice. Planned to stay at the cottage for the weekend, but we both knew by the time we got here that it wasn't enough. By now we're married and you needn't try to find us. We'll be in touch.

Love, Benji

P.S. Wish us luck—we'll need it.

Two hours later they were at each other's throat again. The stalemate had not lasted past the first few accusations as James defended his sister and blamed Benji and Bliss told him angrily that his precious little sister had not been abducted, after all, but had been a willing partner from start to finish.

By the time she finished telling him just what she thought of his arrogant, holier-than-thou attitude, she had drained her small store of energy and was ready to weep again, but at the same time just as determined not to. Tears benefited no one and they certainly wouldn't endear her to the coldhearted creature who stood glowering down at her from his superior height.

"Your brother would have been fired from any other business. He's been fiddling the books for months now, and it's just his luck that Morton was willing to give him another chance . . . for your sake, no doubt," he added witheringly. "He's been warned, but that type won't learn. He'll be in over his head before you know it, and this time he'll drag Leigh down with him!"

The color slowly drained from Bliss's creamy complexion and she took on a look of fragile transparency as the full realization of her brother's activities hit her. Her accusing eyes were enormous pools of dark water, and when James turned to glare at her, his expression changed to one of weary bafflement and he dropped abruptly into his chair. With a sigh of resignation, he said, "Look, it was Morton's idea not to tell you. I don't know exactly what you are to him, but he wouldn't hear of—"

"I'm his cousin! No more, no less, except that when I first came to live with him I was only fourteen and I became his ward! I don't know what you thought, but you certainly made it plain that you suspected the worst from the very first time you barged in on me!"

He shrugged his broad shoulders under the dark gray wool sweater. "My opinion was formed from what I knew of Morton's taste in women and what I saw in the newspapers. As you said, you *were* living with him."

"So was Benji!"

"And that's supposed to be a recommendation?" He lifted one derisive eyebrow, and she clenched her fists in angry frustration. What did it matter what *he* thought of her? The important thing now was Benji.

"How did you find out?" she asked tremulously. "About the books, I mean?"

"It didn't take any great prowess, I assure you. Anyone less blind than Ketchum would have tumbled right away. It's a miracle Morton hasn't been taken greater advantage of with that bookkeeping setup."

"Then it . . . it was not an enormous sum?" she asked fearfully.

"Peanuts. That was only a beginning, though. Given time, he would have dipped in deeper and deeper, having gotten away with it, until he was in over his head, with no hope of recovery."

"But you just said he didn't get away with it," Bliss argued.

"To all intents and purposes he did. No punishment, no scandal. He still has his job, which is pure weakness on Morton's part, as I see it."

"You would! You'd have had him thrown out and called the law after the first penny, wouldn't you? You've no sympathy at all for weakness, have you? Well, whatever mistakes he's made, it's too late now for you to wash your hands and let him go to jail without hurting your sister. You'd better begin to learn how to make the best of it! You must know I'm just as miserable about my new in-law as you are! Make that plural!"

He eyed her speculatively. "I'll take that remark as you no doubt intended I should, as you don't know my sister well enough to judge."

She had the grace to look slightly ashamed, but she didn't withdraw the comment. She didn't like the man and there was no point in pretending she did. "You don't really know Benji, either," she said after the silence had grown uncomfortable. "He may be spoiled, but he isn't a crook. He was barely eighteen when Mama and Daddy were lost, and he didn't ever cry . . . he couldn't get his grief out in the open. But that was when he began to drink and . . . well, to run wild. Oh, he's not an alcoholic or anything like that, and he doesn't use drugs. But he had to get it out of his system, and Morton . . . well, Morton's a dear and I love him very much, but he was no use to Benji as a . . . a father figure."

"Is that what he is to you?" James asked disbelievingly.

For a minute, Bliss looked disconcerted. "I don't know," she said slowly. "I've never really thought about it. He's just . . . Morton. He was there when we needed him and he's never failed us."

James was silent for a long time after that, and Bliss grew uncomfortable under his appraising stare. Whatever was going through his mind wouldn't solve the dilemma that faced them now. Finally she asked, "Isn't Leigh underage?"

"She turned eighteen last week. Probably what they've been waiting for," he added bitterly. "And before you have to ask, yes, there are quite a few places within driving distance where they can be married without too long a wait. The trouble is, we have no way of knowing just which way they were headed."

"And even if we did know, we couldn't do anything about it," she tacked on dolefully, glancing out the window into the impenetrable night.

This particular train of thought led directly to another problem. There was only one bed, and there were two of them. She eyed him warily until he raised a questioning brow at her. "What is it this time?" he asked.

"The bed," she blurted out. "I mean, there's only one and . . . well, I won't sleep with you. You'll just have to stay downstairs."

"In a pig's eye! I'm not freezing myself just so you

71

can lie up there in solitary comfort. You slept with me last night; you can do it again tonight and every night until we can get away from this blasted place!"

She jumped to her feet and confronted him, her eyes sparkling dangerously. "I didn't *know* I was sleeping with you last night! If I had, I assure you, you'd have found yourself out of here fast enough! This is Morton's house and you have no business here. Unless you promise me you'll stay downstairs tonight, you can just take your chances on the road! It won't bother me one bit if you sink up to your elbows in the mud and stay that way until the spring thaw sets in!"

"At which time I'd settle in up to my eyebrows." A gleam of light struck his craggy features and it almost looked as if he were smiling. But Bliss was too much on her guard to be taken in by any momentary softening of his grim visage.

"Wear your coat, then, and keep the fire going. You won't freeze."

"No, but you might. We've enough logs for another few hours, and after that it's a matter of slogging out into the rain to see what we can find and then drying it out enough to burn. Not very encouraging, is it?"

When she didn't answer, he continued, but in a less hard tone. "Have you considered that we may be here for several days? And the chance that we're in for a hard freeze is pretty good this time of year . . . if not tonight, then tomorrow night."

Wordlessly, she stood up, looking around her in almost a dazed fashion. There was no place to run, no place to seek help. She was stuck here with this man, and the only possible way to get through the next few days was to make the best of it if it killed her. "All right. I give up. But you'll wear your clothes, and I will, too," she warned him before turning to plunge their bowls into the cold dishwater in the soapstone sink.

Behind her, James laughed, but it was not an unkind laugh this time. "Worried about what your young man might think?" he asked, getting up to pour water from the steaming kettle into her dishwater.

She looked up at him blankly. "You mean Reade?" she asked after a slight pause. For a moment there her mind had ceased to function and she couldn't think what young man he was referring to.

"The one who had dinner with you at Morton's the other night, the one I've seen squiring you dutifully around town," he supplied.

"That was Reade. He's not . . . well, in a way, I suppose he is, but . . ."

"I think I see," he said dryly. "I wondered about Morton's attitude. For a fellow who's in love with a girl, he allows you too much latitude."

Shocked, she whirled around. "Don't be ridiculous! Morton's not the least bit in love with me! Why, I'm . . . I'm like a . . . a niece to him! I explained that!"

"So you did, so you did; but, knowing women, I'm sure you're well aware of your power over him. Believe me, he doesn't look at you as if you were his niece, or his ward, or his cousin, either," he said acidly. "Nor does he dress you as if you were his niece." His eyes dropped to her rumpled suit and high-necked sweater. "Oh, I'm not talking about that very modest little outfit you're wearing now, but what about that topless thing you had on the night I

73

had to rescue you from that lush Pittmann? Don't tell me he bought that for you when he was in an avuncular mood!"

"That topless thing, as you call it, was designed for the new MacHenry line and it was one of the few things in Morton's shop that could be successfully altered for me! In case you hadn't noticed, I'm not exactly the high-fashion type!"

"Oh, I'd noticed, all right, along with every other male within range. A pocket Venus is the proper, or improper, term, I believe. I hope you were satisfied with the reaction you got. MacHenry will be a huge success, I'll wager."

"It was nothing I couldn't have handled perfectly." She was seething. "You just happened along before I had the chance."

"Oh, ho! Don't give me that! I was there, remember? That lush had you backed in a corner and there was no way out! You may be pretty hefty, but you're no match for a determined man."

That stung! She might be well rounded, but she had certainly never thought of herself as hefty, certainly not when two hands could all but span her waist. "My determination can match that of any man I've ever met," she assured him grimly. "I'm not saying he wasn't making a nuisance of himself, but I would have dealt with him."

"Hmmhmmm," he murmured infuriatingly. Then, as if to defuse the explosive atmosphere, he asked about the years before she had come to live with Morton. More to relieve the tension than for any other reason, she found herself telling him about the years both before and after she had come to live with her cousin. He drew her out so skillfully that she had no way of knowing how very much he learned about Bliss Bonner, the person, as opposed to Bliss Bonner, lovely young socialite seen about town with the dashing Morton Henry.

When the time came when she could no longer stifle her yawns, she eyed him warily. "Do you think there's a chance it might clear up tonight?" she asked wistfully.

"We can hope so, but I wouldn't count on it. Why don't you stop procrastinating and go on up. I'll give you time to get settled and then I'll come along. I won't disturb you, I promise. I don't snore, or so I've been told." He looked at her with an amusement that deepened when the color flooded her face.

What seemed like hours later, Bliss was still wide awake. She was even more awake now than she had been when she had made her reluctant way up the ladder, leaving James staring up after her, a drink in his hand and an undecipherable expression on his face. Beside her now, he breathed with a deep regularity, and Bliss had been acutely conscious of each breath he had drawn since he had slipped quietly in beside her.

She wore her slip and sweater, having rinsed out her bra and tights. They now hung in the makeshift bathroom, where no doubt they would be dripping still come morning. She wondered, not for the first time, what Morton did without the so-called amenities. For a man she had always considered the epitome of the sophisticate, he had certainly revealed a surprising side of his nature in his choice of a retreat. Or maybe all men, no matter how seemingly civilized, retained that sort of basic primitivism —a thought that she found vaguely disturbing under the circumstances.

Twisting slowly so as not to awaken her bedmate,

75

Bliss tried to alleviate the pressure on her right arm, but there was no way she could move and still keep her back turned to James. Cautiously, she rolled over onto her back. He had evidently moved to the center of the bed after he fell asleep. He was a large man, which meant that Bliss had to hang on to the edge of the mattress with a determined grip to keep from sliding downhill and ending up smack-dab against his imposing body.

She was warm, much warmer than she had been all day. Outside she could hear the sullen sound of frozen rain striking the sides of the house. She knew that the road would be even more impassable tomorrow.

Her sweater was twisted around her rib cage and she tugged at it, trying to straighten out a wrinkle that pressed into her back, when a heavy arm was flung across her stomach. She froze, staring distractedly into the darkness. Should she try to remove it, or would that awaken him? And if she awakened him, then what? There had been not the slightest indication on his part that James thought of her as anything other than a necessary evil. All the same, her mind kept flashing taunting visions of his sensual bottom lip, his eyes that had a way of examining her so that she felt completely revealed before him. Hadn't she seen him in action with Rona MacMurdle? There had been nothing impersonal about the man who had leaned across the table laughing lazily into Rona's heavily fringed eyes. When later on Bliss had seen them dancing together, James had held the girl as if he couldn't get close enough to her.

Oh, shut up, Bliss Bonner! she chided herself silently. Just because you're awake in the middle of the night is no reason for you to indulge in these maudlin fantasies!

"Wha'sa matter, can't you sleep?" James murmured drowsily from beside her, causing her to start and draw as far away as possible. It was as if he had read her mind—a disconcerting thought at best!

"I'm only trying to get my sweater straightened out," she whispered tersely. "Sorry if I woke you."

"No problem. Not much to do *except* sleep, unfortunately, and I can do that as well in the morning as tonight. Take it off."

"I beg your pardon?"

"I said take it off. Your sweater, girl. Good Lord, do you think I haven't been in bed with an unclad woman before?"

That was the last thing Bliss wanted to consider. She was quite certain that he had been to bed with more than he could remember, but this was different and she didn't want to be reminded of any possible similarity. As far as she was concerned, they were simply sharing a space under extenuating circumstances. Either one of them would have done the same with anyone else, rather than risk freezing to death.

She told him as much and he laughed softly, turning his head so that his breath played across her cheek like a seductive summer breeze. "One might even be led to believe you've never been to bed with a man before, Bliss Bonner. Would that be true?"

"That's none of your business!" she snapped, turning her back and further twisting her poor sweater under her.

The hand that had fallen from her stomach when she turned touched her back now and she stiffened, clutching the edges of the mattress to keep from sliding downhill into his arms. Then, with an impatient exclamation, she flung off the covers and sat up, reaching for her shoes with one foot. She would spend the rest of the night in a chair! The warmth couldn't all have dissipated from the fire, for it had been going nicely when she had come upstairs.

"Where are you going?"

"If you aren't gentleman enough to let me have the bed to myself, then I'll leave it to you! I'm going downstairs!" she snapped.

"No, you're not." He spoke as calmly as if he were telling her she was losing a hairpin. She jerked away from the hand that had closed over her arm and stood up. She got as far as the door before he caught her and threw her back on the bed, holding her there forcibly with the weight of his body as he landed on top of her.

"You would have to go and bring sex into this debacle! Women! Were you afraid I was only waiting for you to go to sleep so as to have my way with you?" he mocked. "When the time comes that I'm reduced to taking a woman who despises me, I'll give you fair warning. Until then, you're absolutely safe!"

"Since it's perfectly clear to both of us that we despise each other, then why won't you leave me alone and let me sleep downstairs? What difference does it make to you whether or not I freeze to death!"

"On second thought, maybe I ought to determine just exactly how far your antipathy toward me goes. When it comes right down to it, you've no reason to despise me, have you? I've never done anything to you."

Frightened now, she tried to gauge his mood. In the darkness, there was nothing she could see. But she was overwhelmingly aware of the hard weight of his body, even though he was leaning slightly to one side, resting partly on one arm, with both her wrists clasped tightly in one of his large hands. "You're crazy," she hissed at him, struggling vainly to escape. "I hate you!"

"Ah, but that's another matter altogether, my dear Bliss. Hating and despising are worlds apart," he growled softly, a hint of laughter making his voice even more ominous.

"I . . . I don't know what you mean, and I'm not your dear anything! You have no idea what, if anything, I feel about you, so why don't you leave me alone!" There was a tearful note in her voice that made her furious. She bit her lip in an effort to steady a chin that was threatening to crumple.

"Shall I teach you something about yourself, Bliss Bonner?" James asked softly, his words abrading her raw nerves despite their velvet quality. Without waiting for her answer, he slipped a hand beneath her, turning her to face him, and then he pulled her close against his warm, virile body.

Bliss hadn't a chance; what with the eiderdown catching under her and her own clothes twisting and riding up, she was effectively pinned down, subject to the whims of a man she had every reason to distrust, to despise—a man whose very touch was having a disastrous effect on her senses. In the stygian blackness of the room, she was vitally aware of his every move. When his face came closer and closer, it was as if every cell in her body were on standby alert. Just before his lips closed over hers, he laughed softly and she felt it along her spine and gave a small, resigned moan as she was drawn relentlessly into his embrace.

Nothing about her relationship with Reade had ever prepared her for such an all-out assault on her senses and she was lost almost before the battle began. With masterly accomplishment, James Etchison moved his lips sensually over hers, demanding and securing her response. When she felt his tongue begin its insidious explorations, felt his hand slide up under her sweater to capture the throbbing softness of her breast, she was lost to all reason.

With the consummate ease of a man who calculates the effect of every movement, James brought her to the point of complete helplessness, the point where she was kneading her fingers into the firmly muscled flesh beside his backbone. She was all but devastated by the physical manifestations of his desire, and when he lifted his mouth from her lips and she felt the warm, moist caress of his tongue on her aching breast, she could only plead with him for something that was beyond her comprehension. "Please, James . . . ahhhh, please," she whispered tremulously, her head thrown back as she writhed beneath the shuddering sensations that racked her body.

He stared down at her in the darkness; she could feel his eyes on her bare body. Her sweater had gone and she didn't even remember when he had removed it. "Tell me now, Bliss," he murmured against her throat, "tell me how much you hate me."

Her mouth formed the words but no sound came. Something inside her shattered into a million piercing shards and she came down to earth in a free-fall that left her all but mindless.

"You see, Bliss Bonner, I know far more about you than you know about yourself, so don't throw out any more challenges. For lack of something better to do, I just may take you up on them."

So saying, James turned his back on her, and within minutes his breathing had returned to normal. Bliss lay there, physically ill, nauseated at the knowledge that a man, a man she hated, had such power over her body.

Chapter Five

Sometime during the night she must have slept, because much later she remembered opening her eyes to a thin veil of gray light that lay across the carpet of dust on the floor. Beside her James was sleeping on his back, and it occurred to her that even in his sleep he was so in control of himself that there was no relaxing of that firm, thrusting jaw.

She slid out of bed and found her shoes, taking them out to the tiny landing before putting them on to descend the ladder. She had to have time to herself, time to brace herself to meet him in the clear, cold light of day, to face him down and prove to him that no matter what he thought to the contrary, she was totally unmoved by his nearness.

The living room smelled of dead ashes, echoing the taste in her mouth. She had to break a thin film of ice on the water in the basin, and even as she stirred the paper-thin crust with her blue fingers, an idea was forming in her head, gradually taking form with no conscious effort on her part.

It took only a few minutes to determine that the road was frozen into a rutted, downhill course, one that with any luck at all she might be able to negotiate. Once she reached the motorway, she would be off and running if she could only handle her car over the rugged hills and gullies that had frozen into a horrible, rocky, curving track. Not even bothering to grab a bite to eat, she threw on her still-damp clothes, pulled her coat on and grabbed up her purse. She was still grinding impotently at the starter when the door to the cottage opened to reveal a bare-chested James. He leaned indolently against the jamb, idly tossing something up and down in his hand. "Were you needing this?" he called out cheerfully.

"Did you do something to my car?" she demanded accusingly, giving up and climbing out in the face of an utter lack of cooperation from her engine.

"I only removed it for safekeeping. Here, catch!" He tossed the thing and she caught it clumsily, almost stumbling over a frozen clod of mud. She frowned at it, then turned to look doubtfully at her small car. "Where does it go?"

"Oh, I'm sure you can figure that out . . . eventually."

"Why, you . . . you . . ."

He shrugged and turned away.

The weak, watery sun caught the faint touch of silver in his hair and Bliss was sorely tempted to throw the thing at him, but she might need it later. She *would* need it later, just as soon as she could prevail upon him to relent and install it again . . . whatever it was.

Breakfast was a silent meal, with Bliss glowering helplessly and James chatting desultorily about the hiking in the district. "We're not all that far from Yorkshire Dales National Park, I believe. I understand it's possible to walk from Ilkey to Kettlewell, but I wouldn't care to try it in this weather."

"If you won't, then I will!" she snapped at him. Anything to escape the disastrous effect he had on her poise.

"What's the matter . . . sulking? Why, I wonder?"

"As if you didn't know!"

"Oh, you mean last night. Or was it because I tampered with your car!" He watched her closely. "No . . . it was last night, then. Come on, Bliss, don't tell me you've never been made love to before," he jeered softly.

Color flamed in her face and she stood abruptly, gathering up the few dishes and slamming them down again while she reached for the kettle that simmered on the burner. Her angry movements rebounded on her when she splashed boiling water out on her arm. She clutched it, throwing her head back as tears of pain and frustration forced their way from beneath her tightly closed lids.

"Let me see it," James said tiredly from behind her. At his touch, she jerked away.

"Leave me alone," she ordered, enunciating each word desperately. When she heard him slam out the door, her tears began to fall in earnest. But by the time he returned some forty-five minutes later, with a few very damp logs for the fire, she had recovered. She sat huddled in her chair, blowing on her fingers as she stared miserably into the darkened fireplace with its pitifully small pile of coals.

After lunch, James went out again. It was as if he could no longer stand to remain in the tiny room with her, and she was terribly self-conscious whenever she remembered last night—which was almost constantly! He was no doubt laughing at her, gloating over what an abject fool he had made of her. Well, there just might be a way she could retaliate. She had noticed when she made the bed that he had taken the things from his pockets before he went to bed last night. As far as she knew, he had not bothered to replace them. It was not as if there was any use here for small change, a billfold—or car keys, for that matter.

Bliss did not allow herself time to reconsider. She was up the ladder, taking a good look out the tiny window while she was there, and back down again within minutes. Oddly enough, it was only as she was closing the front door after her that she realized she had not given Benji and Leigh a single thought since sometime yesterday.

The Maserati started up like a charm, but Bliss stared in consternation at the gearshift. Somehow, it was a world away from the sturdy little Mini she had driven since her eighteenth birthday. She took a deep breath and raised her eyes heavenward as she threw the thing into first.

The engine sounded like a giant swarm of angry bees and she experienced a moment's hesitation at the feel of all that ferocious horsepower under her small hand, but she was already headed down the steep, rutted road. It was trickier than she had thought; the sun, weak though it was, had thawed the surface of the muddy corrugations. The road was even more slick than it might have been, and the freeze didn't seem to have gone deep enough to make a firm bed. The heavy car broke through the ice puddles as she wrestled against the coercion of eroded ruts on the steep grade, and as she approached the sharpest curve she began applying the brakes gingerly.

When she geared down, it seemed as if the engine were racing, but then she wasn't used to that many cylinders, or whatever the difference was. When she felt the sideways movement, she reached uncertainly for the handbrake and twisted the wheel with her other hand. Something wasn't working right and she had the sickening idea it was herself. But that was all the time she had to think as the car lurched, hesitated for a moment, then, with increasing speed, began sliding toward the rocky outcropping that had been responsible for the curve in the first place. She braked frantically and futilely, and just before the sickening crunch came, she closed her eyes and covered her face with both hands. Even so, the jolt shook her up and her forehead made a rather sudden contact with the windscreen before she could brace herself.

It was not a very noisy crash. It was almost gentle, as crashes go, just a moderate, deliberate meeting of one right front fender with a few tons of solid rock. It didn't even look that bad until she knelt and saw how the metal was bent under against the tire, making it impossible for the car to move.

She could have bawled. She would have liked to sit right down in all that mud and empty, dismal landscape and cry her eyes out from pure disappointment. She had been so close to escape. Now, as bad as things had been, she had succeeded in making them a hundred times worse with one single, impulsive action. And she was not a person given to impulsive actions.

It was that man, of course. That impossible James Etchison! If he had not goaded her into doing something so foolish, she wouldn't be here almost a mile away from the cottage—an uphill mile, at that—from the cold comfort of a barren, primitive cottage that should have been condemned years ago!

But it was not the cottage she dreaded facing again; it was James. It was bad enough to be on the receiving end of his disapproval before, when she had had the satisfaction of righteous indignation in knowing herself blameless in the affair of Benji and Leigh. But now she was in the wrong; she had deliberately stolen his car and tried to run away and wrecked the thing. All those hundreds of pounds worth of expensive machinery tilted gracelessly against a boulder in the wilds of Yorkshire Wolds. Well she couldn't expect to get off lightly.

With nothing to gain by procrastination, Bliss started walking. It was an awkward business at best, and before she had even reached the road again, she had fallen twice and was covered in mud from head to toe. She looked down at the soft, handwoven Irish tweed and the utterly ruined cashmere and groaned. As for her buttery-soft suede coat, it was now a cloddy mess that flapped disconsolately at every step against her laddered hose, dripping into her lizard pumps, one of which got stuck in the mud and had to be pulled out by hand.

The wind whistled down the back of her neck and she tried to remember an old rhyme, something about the wind blowing cold at something on the wold, or was that Cotswold? She was rambling, she reminded herself sternly, picking her way as carefully as she could over the impossible terrain. There had evidently been a good deal of erosion lately, for she didn't remember the road ever being this bad.

Her teeth chattered and she blinked tearfully against the raw, wet wind as she rounded the final turn and saw her own little Mini sitting so innocently outside the small rock building. She railed inwardly at the man who was responsible for this whole miserable state of affairs. If he hadn't taken the part from her own car . . . It was *his* fault that she had had to take the Maserati, his fault that she had had too much car to control as she went down the road, and he wasn't going to get away with blaming her for it!

She threw open the door and yelled at him: "James Etchison, if you say one word, I'm going to kill you! Lethally, willfully *murder* you!" And then she burst into tears.

This time there were no comforting arms to support her, no soft words murmured against her hair. Instead, he closed the door and led her gingerly over to the fire, keeping as much distance between them as he could manage as he peeled her coat from her shoulders. Her cheeks were burning from the warmth after being exposed to the icy blast of the wind. When she stopped sobbing to glare at him from the tangled cover of her fallen hair, she saw that he was barely able to restrain his mirth, and that was the last straw. She swung a fist, and to her amazement it connected solidly with the corner of his mouth.

James's hand came up slowly and touched the place, where a small trickle of blood appeared. When he lowered his hand, there was a smear of mud as well.

Bliss stared, aghast. "Oh, no," she moaned, and then she sneezed four times in rapid succession. James pushed her down into the chair and began removing her shoes, and then he stood her up and reached for the button at her waist.

"What are you doing?" she demanded fiercely, backing away.

"You can't stay in those things, Bliss. There are only two chairs in the place and I'm not about to let you muddy up both of them. Look at the one you were just in. See what I mean?" he demanded. "Now, get undressed and I'll find something for you to wrap up in while I get your bath ready. If nothing else, there's a rug in my car." And then he gazed at her heavily. "Where did you leave it?"

She took a deep breath and looked him balefully in the eye, hardly even flinching when she told him what had happened and then dared him to say one word. "Just don't say *anything!* I don't want to hear a *word!*"

At the corner of his mouth, where, to her shame, a thin line of dried blood still showed, a muscle twitched. Something flickered in his eyes and then was gone and he said, "Get undressed. I'll bring in the tub and fill it. While you're soaking some of the real estate off, I'll fetch sheets, a tablecloth or something that will preserve your modesty."

"There's no tub."

"There's something that will serve once I empty the firewood out of it. Granted, it might leak a bit, but we can mop up afterward. If you tuck your knees right up under your chin, we just might manage to cram all of you in it."

"If there's any cramming to be done, I'll do it," she told him positively, turning her back to unbutton her skirt. She waited until he had left the room before slipping it over her hips and was chagrined to find that her slip was muddy, too. Even if they had been clean before, by the time she had finished removing her tights and sweater there were dark fingerprints everywhere.

The water was almost worth it all, deep, hot and lightly scented from Morton's shaving soap. She settled deliciously into the oval copper boiler, hoping her hips wouldn't jam against the narrow sides when she tried to get out again. She managed to rinse the mud from her hair by dint of extraordinary contortions. When she heard the back door open and close again, signaling James's return from outside, she snatched up the towel he had put there for her and held it in front of her defensively.

There was no door between the living room and the kitchen and she could only hope he was gentlemanly enough to keep his back turned while she dried off and covered herself decently in the top sheet he had provided. Whether or not she would be able to resurrect her clothing was yet to be seen; she had visions of driving all the way back to London draped in a sheet that had seen better days.

She sneezed again, and before she could recover herself, James brought in something steaming and fragrant. He pushed her down into the chair he had wiped clean while she scrambled madly to secure her toga. It was definitely not the warmest of wear!

From the picket fence of drying logs leaning across the hearth, James selected two and added them to the fire. He had evidently discovered a supply while he was outdoors.

"Wow!" she wheezed, dropping her spoon. "What is it?"

"Tinned chicken soup, well laced with onion, garlic, pepper and brandy," he told her, a crooked grin making him appear much younger and not nearly so formidable. "Preventive medicine, my girl. After which you'll be tucked warmly into bed, and sometime before daybreak, barring a sudden thaw, we'll head for home, provided that toy vehicle of yours can straddle the ruts and gullies."

Bliss considered several retorts as she stared at him. The idea of going home was overwhelmingly welcome, wasn't it? It was certainly preferable to spending another single minute here in isolation with a man who was continually throwing her off balance in a way she couldn't begin to understand.

"No comment?" he asked, stacking bowls and refilling mugs.

"Would any comment of mine make a difference?" she parried.

"Does that mean you aren't all that anxious to leave here anymore?"

"You know very well I am! If nothing else, I proved that to you!"

He grinned again, far too disarmingly for her peace of mind. "I wonder just why you thought you had to prove it to me. Or just what you were running away from," he mused.

She told him very frankly that she had been running away from him and his beastly temper, but even as she spoke she wondered if she was being quite honest with herself. It was not his temper that kept her aware of his every movement, his every look. Nor was it the harsh words he had spoken to her that she remembered as she made her way up the ladder several minutes later.

She had wanted to empty the tub but James had forestalled her. So, while she cleared away the few supper things and then finished up in the bathroom, he dumped the water out by the bucketful. By the time she was ready for bed, the tub was turned upside down on the sink.

"Well . . . good night," she said tentatively, tugging the sheet more closely about her. She considered sleeping on the two chairs and waking in the night to replenish the fire, but she knew that at any such suggestion James would simply throw her across his shoulder and carry her upstairs. Her dignity had already suffered enough without being treated like a sack of coal.

Besides, he had proved pretty conclusively that he didn't fancy her, not that way or any other way. She secured the ends of her makeshift toga and lifted the skirts to reveal an old pair of Morton's bedroom slippers she had found in the bathroom, and then tackled the ladder.

She felt sorry for all the ancient Egyptians if later generations made them turn in their graves, because the feat was virtually impossible for one wrapped from head to toe in yards and yards of linen. A restless sleeper under the best of conditions, Bliss was in misery long before the first gray fingers of light touched the window. She had been dozing lightly when James came up. Although she was awake, she pretended to be asleep when he eased his large body in beside her. But try as she would, she could not keep from sliding down the incline caused by their unequal weight. It was either give up the struggle to keep herself decently covered and hang on to the edge of the mattress, or let herself go and snuggle up cozily against that solid, reassuringly warm back.

Unfortunately, while she was asleep she did both, and when she stirred again, it was to find herself held fast in a pair of oak-hard arms while James's soft, even breath stirred the golden-tipped tendrils about her face. She lay there for several long moments, feeling all sorts of peculiar, delightful and absolutely forbidden sensations course through her body. It was only when she tried to ease herself away that he stirred beside her.

Those eyes, had she ever found them cold? Impossible! They opened and after only a split second of confusion smiled with slow, warm realization into her own. "Good morning," he said, the words sliding softly across the few inches of pillow that separated their faces.

"Would you please move your arm?" she asked a little desperately.

He seemed to consider her request for a moment. "No, I don't think so."

"James! Please."

"It occurs to me, belatedly, that I should have taken a long, strenuous hike last night instead of coming to bed. It seems I've overestimated my strength of character."

"James," she said warningly, wriggling to free herself, only to have his arm drop from her shoulder to her waist and haul her up against him again. She was frightfully, dangerously aware of the electrifying feel of his legs against hers, the springy softness of his hair against the satin smoothness of her own skin. When his knee inserted itself between her thighs and he pulled her half over on top of him, she panicked and began to push herself away.

He ignored her protests as if it were all a huge game. "Did you know you're particularly beautiful when you wake up? No cracked hair lacquer, no smudges of makeup . . . just a sort of dewy-fresh, soft-focused innocence. How do you do it, hmmm? You could make a fortune if you could patent it."

With her elbows braced against his chest, she strained against the arms that held her down easily. "You're absolutely insane, did you know that? I don't know what sort of women you're used to waking up with, and I'm not interested in knowing! Just let me—"

"Aren't you? That's another surprise, then, in a long list of surprises." He pulled her head down and forced her mouth to touch his, but she was determined that the touch should not become a kiss and she kept her lips clamped tightly shut until she felt his laughter shaking the bed. Then, outraged as well as frightened at her own traitorous responses, she opened her mouth to protest and he pounced.

The kiss was like nothing she had ever experienced before, an exercise in joyous sensuality that left her utterly defenseless. When he smiled into her eyes and told her he wanted to make love to her, she groaned and dropped her face into his throat. "Oh, James, you're not being fair. Please, please, don't do this to me."

With mock innocence, he stared up at her. "Bliss, have I done anything you didn't want me to? Have I taken—"

"Taken advantage? You know you have! I wanted

to stay downstairs last night . . . I wanted *you* to, at least, but you promised me—"

"Darling, all promises go overboard when a man wakes up to discover a beautiful woman in his bed. How could you honestly expect me to act any differently? May I remind you that in your own weakened condition, after yesterday's ordeal, it would seriously undermine your chances for recovery if you tried to fight against the body's natural inclination?"

She tilted her head and stared at him, half in anger, half in reluctant amusement. "You're utterly out of your head, did you know that? Even half asleep, you come up with the most plausible line any man could feed a girl. It won't work, you know. My resistance may or may not be weakened by yesterday's mudbath, but I've better sense than to believe any line of drivel you please to hand out."

The warm light of amusement that had flickered in his eyes was suddenly eclipsed as his pupils grew large and darker. "I can feel your heart going like a trip-hammer, Bliss. Your eyes have that look that tells me you want me as much as I want you, so it must be something else. Is it Reade? Are you wondering how he'll take it if he discovers you've been with another man?"

A wave of pain washed over her. He sounded as if he thought she made a practice of sleeping with men. She managed to pull away from his relaxed grip, but he caught the trailing edge of the sheet that still clung to her body and held her there.

"Bliss? Are you really a girl with old-fashioned morals, then? That's a little hard to believe, considering the circles you move in."

"You know nothing at all about me, James

Etchison! You have no right to judge me according to your own sleazy standards—and as for morals, did it ever occur to you that I just might not be tempted? Women are different from men. We don't just drop into bed on the slightest pretext, and it may come as a shock to you, but you're not altogether irresistible, you know!" All the time she was protesting, she knew with a horrible certainty that she was lying in her teeth. The only thing that prevented her from giving in to his demands was the knowledge that, for him, it was all a lighthearted game, a sort of musical beds routine with no meaning beyond the purely physical enjoyment. That thought was to haunt her for a good time to come. Now, as the knowledge of how very much she wanted him to make love to her sank in, she could only stare into his measuring eyes, her own eyes large with confused emotions.

Softly, he said, "Another challenge, girl? I think your mind and your body are having one hell of a fight right now, and it just might amuse me to tip the scales. Shall I?"

She drew back, but she was not fast enough. His hands closed over her shoulders and toppled her back down on his chest. Then, before she could recover her balance, he had rolled over on her, so that she was held captive, her heart pounding in her throat with a frantic, suffocating wildness. The one thin layer of fabric that separated their bodies might just as well not have been there for all the difference it made. When Bliss's fingers moved through the hair on his chest, pushing urgently against him, they encountered the pinpoints of his nipples and she gasped at the immediate reaction of his body against her own.

Her eyes were still open, as were his, when he

came closer and touched the line between her lips with the tip of his tongue. As she felt her last weak defense fall away she opened to him and allowed herself to be possessed by the overwhelming sensuality of his kiss.

There was no contest; circumstances were against her and James was too skilled in the art of making love. When she felt his hands trace the inward curve of her waist, moving the sheet away as they dropped down lower, she was lost. She was one fierce, pulsating mass of need. Even while something inside her was screaming silent warnings, she was tracing the hard warmth of his body with her trembling fingers, glorying in the realization of what her touch was doing to him, thrilling to the pounding of his heart against her own and inhaling the scent of his musky, healthy masculinity.

Her mind raced frantically, filled with seemingly random thoughts. Why was she allowing this to happen when there was no question of anything deeper than a momentary gratification between them? Didn't they heartily dislike each other? Didn't they distrust and even despise each other? What was it James had said last night about not being reduced to the level of taking a woman who despised him? Or had it been one he despised? And if he didn't despise her now, how would he feel afterward, when they returned to London and their families?

Their families. "James, no!" She made one last desperate effort to free herself, clutching at a straw as she felt herself about to go down for the third time. "Benji and Leigh . . . this is what you hated for your own sister, isn't it? Isn't it?" she pleaded, "Then how can you do this to me?" It took the last thin thread of sanity to hold back when all in the world she wanted was to give James everything he asked of her. But some vestige of self-preservation whispered that that way lay more pain than she was capable of bearing.

Muscles that had been pliant a moment before hardened as he froze, and just for an instant she saw his passion-darkened eyes flicker warily before they became shuttered. "I was under the impression that this was a joint effort," he said, his voice husky, but steady nonetheless.

"You know that's not true . . . at least . . ." she whispered, breaking off in confusion at the expression she saw on his face. It took several moments for her turbulent emotions to subside to the point where she could begin to think constructively. During that time, her stricken eyes did not leave his face, taking in the fine stubble that shadowed his angular jawline, the lines that traced their way down his lean cheeks from his proud nose to the outer corners of his firm, deeply chiseled mouth. "James . . . please . . . we both know you've made your point. You're experienced enough to bring any woman to her knees, given circumstances like these. But you can't act one way and speak another. You were so concerned for Leigh, thinking she was here alone with Benji. That was what brought you here in the first place, remember?"

He rolled over onto his back, staring up at the moisture-mottled ceiling, stained from past leaks. In her anxiety, Bliss reached out and touched his shoulder. He jumped away as if her fingers were thorns.

"I'm sorry," she apologized, not really understanding why she should, and in her concern not caring. "But, James, you must know it's true. You were treating me the way you were afraid Benji was treating Leigh, and I . . . I'm someone's sister, too."

"Shut up! Just be quiet, will you?" he exploded. "Get dressed! We're getting out of here right now, and if your car won't make it, then we'll walk! If there's one thing I can't stand, it's a woman who doesn't know when to let well enough alone! Your precious virtue is safe, isn't it?"

The drive home was one of the most uncomfortable Bliss had made in her life, and not just because of her stiff and muddy clothes. James drove with a maniacal fury, although she gradually came to realize that the control he exerted over his own temper was extended to the car, as well. Oddly enough, even when he terrified her, she trusted him implicitly. As she sat beside him, uncomfortably aware of the potent masculine force he exuded, she felt all her animosities drain away. That in itself was frightening. She knew with certainty that James Etchison had made an indelible impression on her life. She would never again be able to trust her own reactions, at least not with a man. At least, not with a man like James—but there *were* no other men like James, she thought with a sad resignation. Better the anger she had felt for the first few hours than this thing that was stealing insidiously into her heart.

She risked a sidelong glance at him an hour after he had stopped and brought her a sandwich and a mug of tea from a pub. He had been perfectly in control, just as he always was. Not for one minute, she thought with bitterness, had he been unable to direct his emotions with that computerlike brain, no matter how far gone in passion he might pretend to be.

But some things couldn't be pretended, she reminded herself. He had been aroused almost to the point of no return; even in her own inexperience, she had instinctively recognized that fact. But then, he *had* controlled the situation, hadn't he? She made herself accept the fact that James cared no more for her now than he had the first time he had burst in on her. She had been, to all intents and purposes, available. She had been in his bed, or he in hers, and what more could she have expected of him?

Passion! The whole thing was probably just a case of tit for tat, an attempt to score against her brother. If there had been one or two moments of tenderness during the past thirty-six hours, they were no doubt as well planned as the rest of his actions. They had been calculated for effect, she told herself as some vestige of self-preservation made her throw up a barrier against her own weakness. The less she saw of James Etchison in the future, the better she would like it! Let him go back to his precious Rona; she was more his speed—hard, polished and completely self-seeking. Let them bounce off each other's gold-plated surfaces. She herself preferred someone more . . . more like Reade, she told herself in desperation, gathering up her purse as they turned into Morton's street.

It was teatime when they pulled up in front of the narrow, three-story white house. Bliss got out stiffly, not waiting for James to assist her. Until this moment it had not occurred to her that he had no way to get to his own home unless he came in with her to call a cab. And she didn't want him with her, not even for that long.

"I'll return your car in an hour or so and find out any news you might have of the children," he called after her, not getting out from under the wheel.

Without so much as a by-your-leave! she thought illogically. Just take what you want and never mind the inconvenience to anyone else!

Without a word, she marched up to the door and fumbled in her bag for her key, only to have the door flung open for her by Morton himself. His eyes took in Bliss's pitiful state of dishevelment and moved on immediately to where James still lingered in the Mini. While he was pulling Bliss inside with one hand, he exclaimed, "Good God, what happened to you two? James, you'd better come inside, too."

Martha was waiting anxiously in the foyer. Bliss's impulse was to fly to her plump, confortable arms, but there was to be none of that. Morton, with James right behind him, took her by the arm and steered her into his study, where she confronted a tableau that was to remain imprinted on her consciousness for a long time to come.

Leigh and Benji sat close together on the brocaded regency sofa, its very formality emphasizing their youthful defensive demeanors. Benji's arm was around Leigh's shoulder and both sets of eyes were wide with a touching sort of belligerence. It was not to these two that her stricken gaze went, however, but to Rona MacMurdle. The tall, cool blonde was draped in a graceful pose on the matching sofa, and in this case the woman and the setting were made for each other. Rona might have dressed for the scene, so perfectly did she blend with the muted elegance of the room. The only expression that was allowed to mar the porcelain perfection of her features was one of slight, well-bred distaste as she took in Bliss's stiff, filthy clothes, her ruined shoes and the wild mop of unbrushed waves that surrounded her face.

"Great Scott, what happened to you?" she drawled mere seconds before her eyes lighted on James.

Bliss could almost claim to have been amused, watching the dawning realization creep into those pale blue, lushly lashed eyes as Rona looked from James to Bliss and back again. But the hardening that took the place of amused speculation was utterly chilling.

There was a flurry of voices, all speaking at once. James strode across the room, ignoring everyone but Leigh. When he would have taken his sister in his arms, the child clung to Benji.

"We're married, Jimmy. We were married this morning and there isn't a thing you can do about it," she challenged, clinging to Benji with a stubborn determination that surprised Bliss.

"Oh, no?" growled James. "You don't have to stay married to him, Leigh. We can have it annulled and you can come home with me and forget the whole ugly mess." He reached for her again, and something sparked in the girl's face.

"It's too late for an annulment, Jimmy, and anyway, why won't you understand that Benji and I love each other? Not everyone is like you and Celine, you know. Benji and I . . . well, unless you want your nephew to be born without a family, you'd better get used to the fact that we're going to stay married," Leigh finished in a defiant rush of words.

For the first time since she had known him, Bliss felt truly sorry for James Etchison. The color drained from his face, leaving him ashen and so utterly vulnerable that it was all she could do not to throw her arms around him and try to shield him from what had hurt him so deeply.

Into the crystal silence that followed Leigh's revelation, Benji spoke. "I'm sorry for leading you such a chase, Bliss. It's just that one thing led to another and . . . well, we knew we had to get married." As a slow stain crept under his skin, he continued. "Not in that sense, you understand. I mean, well, we did, but . . . I love her and she loves me and nobody's going to break us up."

"I understand, Benji," Bliss told him. She turned to Leigh. "If there's anything I can do to help . . ."

And then Rona spoke, reminding them all that quite a lot of family linen had been aired before a stranger. "Well, I must say, you look as if you've had one hell of a chase. What kept you two, anyway?" The words were spoken in a brittle, bright voice, but when James answered her, there was no lightness at all in his tired tones.

"The rain, chiefly," he told her. "That and the fact that we didn't have a clue where to turn next."

"You mean you've been at the cottage since Friday night?" Morton asked, looking from one to the other as his face took on a look that defied description.

"But . . . but there's only the one room there," Benji joined in.

Dryly, James observed, "We noticed."

"Well, why didn't you leave when you found out we'd gone?" the younger man persisted angrily.

"Because, you fool, it was pouring and the road

was impassable and your sister wrecked my car! Now, have you any more questions, or shall we just broadcast the whole affair and be done with it?"

Rona stood up with a fluid movement. She touched Morton lightly on the cheek as she crossed to where James stood, his feet braced widely on the silky perfection of the faded old carpet. "Perhaps we'd better make a fast getaway, darling, before poor Morton is forced to drag out the shotgun to protect the family honor. I'm sure they all have lots and lots to talk about, and you, my love, look as if you could do with a stiff drink and maybe a thick steak . . . my specialty, if you'll remember?"

Chapter Six

The newlyweds were installed in a flat which Morton, using some connection left over from his real-estate days, secured for them. For Benji's sake, Bliss made an effort to cultivate a friendship with the younger girl. Aside from feeling sorry for her, she felt a sort of kinship, for weren't they both victims of James's stern disapproval?

She had not seen James at all since that dreadful afternoon when he had driven off with Rona Mac-Murdle, and she told herself she was delighted. Seven months from now, more or less, she might have to share honors with him at a christening. But until then, the less she saw of him, the better she would like it.

Why, then, did she stare after every man she saw with broad shoulders and a lightly frosted head of hair until he turned around? And why did she have that heavy feeling of emptiness inside her when he turned out not to be James Etchison?

Reade came around often, and through sheer defensiveness she allowed herself to drift into an even deeper relationship with him. There was little enough lovemaking, for Reade was not an especially demonstrative man. And for that Bliss was thankful. It was enough to have someone to take her out of herself, someone who might someday block out the memory of a weekend spent with a man whose every look electrified her.

Reade was restful (she would not allow herself to think of him as boring) and she dined and danced with him, and a couple of times she unfolded the morning paper to see their pictures staring at her from the society page. There was also pictures of another couple, once, a couple whose tall, familiar good looks had been snapped while they leaned on a fence at a well-known breeding stable. She knew Josh and Sybil were horsy and she tried to tell herself that James was just accompanying Rona out of courtesy. But it wouldn't wash, especially when more than once she and Reade glimpsed them at a nightclub or a restaurant.

Even now, she found herself watching a couple circle the floor at the supper club and thinking how alike they were to another man and woman—the same sleek, blond beauty, rather stereotyped but nonetheless effective for that, and the same tall, rangy build that moved with surprising grace for one so large. They moved out of the shadowy corner where they had been dancing and under the muted lights, Bliss saw with a painful hollowness that it was James and Rona. Then they both looked up and caught her staring at them.

She turned back to Reade. "What were you saying?" she asked brightly, leaning closer to him as if it were only the noise that had prevented her hearing his words.

"I said I've a client to see at three, but we can go on out and look at the house in the morning. Then, after I get through with Delgado, I'll pick you up and we can have dinner somewhere to celebrate. All right with you?" There was an eagerness in him that made her heart sink, and she found herself, from a variety of confused emotions, agreeing to be picked up at ten on the following Saturday. They left as soon after that as she could manage, and only when they were safely inside Reade's Renault did she allow herself to relax. When she did, her shoulders aching enough to tell her she had been holding them rigidly since she had spotted James and Rona, she felt curiously near tears. So, when Reade would have come in with her for a nightcap, she pleaded a headache and he left, promising to see her in a couple of days.

On Friday afternoon, Morton called from the office to ask her to bring a file he had inadvertently left in his study. Since she had to make the trip, she gathered up several small items she had put aside for Leigh and Benji's flat; Morton's attic had collected a good bit of cast-off furniture through the generations. Bliss was eager to help them out, especially since, without ever having discussed Benji's lapse from grace with him, she sensed in him a new purpose. Leigh tended to be extremely defensive, however, and Bliss was treading warily so as not to offend the young girl. Both Leigh and Benji were determined to make it with no help from anyone, due, she thought bitterly, to James's attitude toward Benji.

Besides, the younger girl seemed to have some strange idea that Bliss was a supersophisticate, a social butterfly who reigned supreme over both Chez Henri and Morton's residence between nightclubs and theater dates. Nothing Bliss had been able to do so far had made a dent in that ludicrous idea, not even the hours she had put in at the flat, scrubbing and painting when Leigh's tricky stomach rebelled.

After dropping off the folder with Max, who met her at the curb in front of the shop, she made her way through heavy traffic to the modest neighborhood where the young Bonners lived. Benji, of course, would still be at work, and she only hoped Leigh would be home. It hadn't occurred to her to call first.

The door was answered after several minutes by a Leigh who looked pale and drawn. Bliss stepped in uncertainly, wondering if she had interrupted a quarrel between the newlyweds. "Is . . . are you all right? Is Benji here?" she asked tentatively. "I've a few things out in the car I thought you might be able to use, since they're only . . ." She broke off, alarmed now at the look in Leigh's huge, frightened eyes. Instinctively, she reached out and caught at her hands. "Leigh, what's wrong? Is it Benji? Are you all right?"

"Yes, I'm . . . oh, no! Bliss, something's wrong! I can feel it . . . in here." She clasped her abdomen, and her tears brimmed over and scattered among the freckles on her beautifully molded face. In jeans and a shirt of Benji's, she looked no more than twelve years old, and Bliss realized, perhaps for the first time, the depths of James's concern. Her every sense alert now, she led the girl over to the sofa and urged her down. "Tell me about it," she implored.

"That's just it," Leigh wailed. "I don't know. . . . It's just a sort of a nagging ache, but I know . . . Bliss, I really *know* something's wrong with the baby!" She was sobbing in earnest by now, and Bliss held her protectively, comfortingly, as her mind raced frantically in search of the answer.

"Who's your doctor? He'll be the one to call. Shall I get him on the phone for you?"

Leigh told her, and Bliss talked to the nurse-receptionist and then to the brisk-sounding man at the other end of the line. Five minutes later she had bundled Leigh into her coat and was driving to the clinic, trying to keep her mind on her driving instead of the distraught girl beside her. Just as she pulled into the parking area, Leigh turned and grabbed her arm, causing the car to swerve dangerously before Bliss got it under control again. "Call Benji, will you? Tell him . . . tell him I need him!"

"I'll call just as soon as I've turned you over to Dr. Rushly," Bliss promised.

"And James," Leigh added.

"You'll be able to call him yourself as soon as you're through here, Leigh," Bliss responded.

"Call him! Tell him I must see him, Bliss. Please!"

Bliss would have promised to summon Saint Peter just to calm the girl down. But when, half an hour later, she dialed the number Leigh had given her, her mouth was dry and her hand none too steady. She had seen James several times since they had returned from Yorkshire Wold, but she had not spoken to him.

She chewed a thumbnail and tapped a small, elegantly shod foot in its rust-colored suede boot while she fancied she could hear the shrill summons echoing through an empty house. When the deep, achingly familiar baritone came on the other end, she was caught speechless.

"Hello!" James demanded irritably for the third time.

"James? It's Bliss. Bliss Bonner."

"I remember you," he mocked. "The girl with mud on her clothes."

Nonplussed, she stammered for a minute, then bit her lips as he laughed. "James, listen to me! I'm calling from Headly clinic . . . it's over near—"

"I know where it is. What's wrong, are you hurt? Ill?" He sounded suddenly tense, almost as if he cared, she thought fleetingly as she tried to find the best way to tell him about his sister.

"No, but I dropped by to see Leigh and she . . . she wasn't feeling quite the thing, and so—"

He interrupted her to say he would be right there and slammed down the receiver. For several moments, Bliss stood holding the phone, staring at it stupidly while in her mind's eye she watched him as he strode out to his black Maserati. He would be pulling on his sheepskin coat as he moved, his hair untidy and that grim, driven look on his face as he lowered himself under the wheel with a terse movement.

Stop it! You're becoming obsessed with the man, just because no one has ever irritated you so, aggravated you more, or made you angrier! Her mind said the words even as her body remembered a breathless, shuddering ecstasy that it had never experienced before, nor would again.

Benji came first, his eyes haunted. When Bliss

could provide him with no answers, he took off down a corridor that was off limits and Bliss didn't even bother to call him back. Let someone else tell him that no one except staff was allowed beyond the green sector. Meanwhile, she sat huddled on a plastic bench and stared blindly at a framed reproduction of several types of poisonous snakes and spiders, a cheerless decoration, to say the least.

"Bliss? How is she?" It was James. He looked harried, but he had himself in tight control. She told him all she knew and watched as a muscle at the side of his jaw tightened, then relaxed again as he offered to buy her a cup of coffee.

They waited for perhaps another fifteen minutes before Benji, his arm holding his wife protectively, followed a white-coated man who was walking down the corridor toward them. Bliss searched their faces, and when Benji grinned at her—a weak effort, but a grin nevertheless—she expelled her breath in a long sigh and allowed her shoulders to droop tiredly. James had stood, and now he drew the doctor aside as Benji and Leigh sat down beside Bliss on the worn bench.

"False alarm," her brother told her, still holding the slight form of his wife tightly to his side. "This little girl's been trying to do too much, what with Christmas almost on us and the flat to do up. Her body's just trying to tell her to knock it off for a spell. Doctor Rushly says if she'll take it extra easy for a few days, then she can sit around and boss me while I put the trimmings on the baby's room."

Leigh's tremulous smile as she gazed up at her young husband did something to Bliss and she found her own eyes brimming over. She fumbled in her bag

111

for a handkerchief and tried to keep her back turned away when James rejoined them. What an end to a day!

"I suggest the two of you get yourselves on home and follow doctor's orders," she told them with slightly damp smile.

"Can you run us home? I came in a cab. Oh, and, Bliss," Benji added, "can I speak to you for a minute?" He led her aside while James helped Leigh on with her coat, and Bliss was mentally counting the money she had on her when he surprised her by asking if she could do him a favor.

"Well, of course I can. Do you need . . . ?"

"Tomorrow I have some extra work at the office. Morton's paying me extra to help with some clerical work, if you can imagine me as a secretary. At any rate, I don't want to leave Leigh alone. Do you suppose you could drop in, accidentally, sort of, and keep her company until I'm free?"

"I'd love to! Maybe I can help with the decorating —that is, unless you two want to do it all your-selves," she suggested.

"Be my guest. I'm no great hand with draperies and suchlike, but unless it gets done, Leigh will be fit to bust. She's a right determined little lady, is my wife, and I intend to see that she stays in bed at least until the middle of the week."

The pride and love in his voice when he spoke of her was unmistakable, and Bliss was fiercely glad that James had approached them in time to overhear the last few words. If he had any more doubts about the rightness of this particular union, surely he was not still harboring them after such a spontaneous demonstration of Benji's care.

They left the clinic together, and James herded the young couple into his own car, leaving Bliss to go home in her Mini. She tossed them a wave but had no idea whether or not anyone saw her—not that it mattered, she told herself, pushing away the tiny empty feeling.

Knowing Benji would be leaving home shortly before nine, Bliss was dressed and ready, her eyes glowing with a sort of subliminal excitement that she could not have explained to herself even had she noticed it. She told Martha where she was going— "to baby-sit for Benji while he puts in a bit of overtime"—and told her not to fix any lunch, for she would probably have a sandwich over at the flat before she came back.

She cut through the park to Bayswater Road and as she neared Paddington she admitted to herself that she was hoping James might choose to drop in and see how his sister was this morning. Last night's episode had been enough to prove to her that she was not over her silly infatuation for him. She refused to call it anything but infatuation, in spite of the fact that he haunted the fringes of her consciousness both day and night. When she pulled up in front of the charming Victorian house where Benji and Leigh had their flat, she lifted her chin imperceptibly against the stab of pain that came when there was no Maserati at the curb, no road-hugging, aggressive mass of machinery to make her heart beat quickly when she let herself in with the key Benji had provided.

"I'm in here," Leigh called out weakly and Bliss followed the voice to the small bedroom. "Benji made me eat a bite before he left me, in case I got to feeling queasy later on," Leigh admitted. "If you don't mind too much, I'm dreadfully sleepy still."

"Best thing in the world for you. I'll just take myself off to the living room and read the morning paper. I missed it at home."

"Move the curtains over, then. I was pressing them yesterday when I began to feel ill."

"Why don't I hang them for you?" Bliss suggested.

"Oh, would you? But I'm afraid they may be wrinkled again now."

"I'll touch them up, then. Really, it will be fun to do. After all, I have a stake in this baby, too, you know."

"I just can't believe it," Leigh said, a glow coming over her sleepy features. "I wish I could peek inside and see if it's a boy or a girl, and whether or not it looks like Benji. It will probably have his reddish hair and my freckles."

"And it will be absolutely adorable. Now close your eyes and don't surface again until lunchtime, all right? Baby needs a nap."

She cleaned up the tiny kitchen first. Whatever her brother's skills as a breakfast chef, he fell far short in other domestic areas. When she finished, she looked in to see that Leigh was fast asleep. Then she tiptoed to the little front room that had been set aside as a nursery, closing the door behind her in case she should disturb Leigh.

The curtains needed a slight touching up with the iron, and as that appliance was still set up from the day before, she did both pairs of ruffled cotton, trying, as she did so, to imagine Benji shopping for something so frivolous as pink rabbits and yellow turtles. There was no ladder, but a kitchen stool sufficed. She was in her stocking feet four feet off the floor with a stubborn curtain rod in one hand and a crisp curtain in the other when she heard someone in the next room.

"If you don't get right back into that bed, I'm coming to put you there myself," she announced through the door, giving the rod one final twist that dropped it into its slot.

"Sounds promising," came the laconic reply from behind and below.

"James!" She whirled around on the stool, missed her footing and clutched at the empty air as she tumbled backward into his waiting arms. The momentum carried James backward in turn, and he collapsed into the sagging overstuffed rocker with Bliss on top of him. When she struggled to get up he held her in place, with one arm around her middle and the other around her shoulders. The hand that gripped her shoulder slipped up beneath her hair and pressed her head down so that she was breathing in the enticing scent of his clean skin and subtle fragrance of his aftershave.

"James," she whispered fiercely, "let me go!"

"For such a little girl, you pack quite a wallop, but then, I should know about that from past experience, hmmm?" He grinned lazily into her eyes, his narrowed, slightly mocking eyes scintillating with gold lights, like a sunset on a stormy sea.

Before she could regain her balance enough to push herself away, he brought her head across slowly until her lips just brushed against his. Raising his other hand to her face, he held her off, then let his eyes rove over her distraught features for a moment. Then he kissed her with a shattering thoroughness that broke through her pitiful defenses and sent them reeling off into the distance. When at last he lifted his mouth from hers, easing away with a series of tiny bites and nibbles until she could have screamed, he studied her again, looking through her eyes into her mind, her heart and soul until she was terrified that he might discover the secret she had been keeping even from herself.

"I needed that," he said quietly, shifting and resetting her on his lap.

She was acutely aware of his body beneath hers, the smooth play of the muscles in his thighs as he stretched his long legs out until they almost reached the opposite wall. He pulled her head down so that it lay against his shoulder and he raked his fingers through her hair. "What have you been doing these past few weeks, besides dining and dancing with the estimable Reade Johnston?"

"Nothing very exciting. James, please let me up."

"Relax. There's nowhere else to sit in here . . . a chair, a chest and a crib. Aren't you comfortable?"

"Yes . . . no . . . that's not the point!"

"Hush! Let's not wake Leigh. I assume she's still sleeping and we're not as apt to disturb her in here. And, Bliss," he added, a different note invading his deep voice, "I appreciate your coming to the rescue yesterday. I think it will be good for Leigh, having another girl about who is her own age."

"I'm not Leigh's age; I'm twenty. But I think I'll like it, too. I've never had a sister before." She could feel the steady beat of his heart beneath her ear, and it had the effect of increasing her own pulse rate as she tried and failed to control the pounding of her own heart.

116

"So," James remarked softly, "you are sisters. Does that make you my sister, as well?"

"Of course not! We're nothing to each other. I really must get up, James. I . . . there are . . ."

He laughed, and the sound triggered off the strangest sensations in the pit of her stomach. "Nothing? I'm beginning to wonder, Bliss Bonner. Every time I think I have you added up just right, the sum changes, another figure is added or subtracted and I have to start all over again. A misplaced penny can drive an accountant wild, Bliss, did you know that?"

He twisted her head around, his well-kept hand clasped firmly on her chin. She could feel his gaze as it touched her mouth, dropped to the frantic pulse at the base of her throat and returned to caress her lips again. It hovered there until she could feel the warm color wash up over her whole body. She slapped his hand away and slithered down until she could get at least one foot on the floor.

"Running away again?" he taunted gently, adjusting the creases in his tailored flannels as she stood up. He was still sprawled in the rocking chair, and Bliss was supremely conscious of the spread of his powerful thighs, the shape of his chest and shoulders under the lightweight woolen jersey. He had tossed his coat on the floor, she now saw, and the sight of that sheepskin garment brought back with compelling intensity her memories of a weekend a month before.

"I'm going to check up on Leigh," she told him, edging away.

"Commendable." He came to his feet with one lithe motion and before she could gain the door, he had barred her way, raising his arm to lean against the wall where she was pinned like a butterfly.

Frantically, she turned in the other direction; he put up his other arm and she was trapped. Then he closed in on her and by the time he brought her up close against his body, she was trembling all over from a wild, unwilling expectancy. "Please, James," she pleaded turbulently.

"I wonder why you're so frightened of me, Bliss Bonner. Surely after spending an entire weekend with me alone you know I'm no threat to you, don't you?" He rubbed the tip of his blade of a nose against her own much smaller one and smiled lazily, insolently, into her eyes.

"I'm not frightened! You don't scare me at all, James! You . . . I . . . it's just that . . ."

"Yes? Do go on."

"Oh, stop playing with me!" She jerked her head away from him and made an effort to duck under his arm. But he tightened his grip, dropping one hand slowly down her spine to curve her hips against him in a way that made her knees buckle. She was devastatingly aware of the threat of his masculinity, the purely physical hold he had over her. Something inside her was crying out for all he offered her and more, far, far more.

When his mouth captured hers again, taunting, teasing, provoking before deepening into an assault that had her clinging helplessly to him, she slid her hands up and down his sides and hips. She was lost and she knew it. She felt the zipper of her bronze-colored jersey slide down, revealing her back to the coolness of the room, and she whimpered against his bedeviling mouth. His lips slipped across her cheek, to follow the tendon down her neck to the hollow of her shoulder. She went wild with the coursing of ripple after ripple of exquisite sensation. Then she felt his hands as they touched the straps of her slip and eased them from her shoulders along with the straps of her bra. When his hands gently cupped her breasts, allowing the turgid nipples to swell between his fingers before he began to tantalize them, she twisted her head helplessly from side to side. "Ahh, James, please . . . don't do this to me," she whispered in a voice she didn't recognize.

"Is this what you're afraid of, Bliss? But it's not me you're afraid of, admit it. It's what we are together," he murmured in her ear, "what we can do for each other."

"We're nothing together," she threw out desperately. "Please, James . . . it's not fair. I'm not . . . I haven't . . . ah!" She dropped her head as she felt his strong teeth on the throbbing peak of her breast.

Then he stood straight, molding her to him so that she knew the fullness of his desire. "I know you aren't, you haven't, love. But that doesn't mean you won't." He kissed her eyes, one after the other. "That's only one of the things about you that doesn't add up," he teased in a voice that had regained some of its usual steadiness. "I should have thought . . ."

They both jumped at the harsh shrill of the door buzzer. James stepped away and hurried to forestall another attack before Leigh was awakened, leaving Bliss to straighten herself out as best she could. She leaned against the wall, drawing in a deep, shaky breath as she resettled her clothing. She felt terribly abandoned, cast aside, discarded, and she tried to tell herself that James had been reluctant to leave her.

But he hadn't. He had begun to draw away from

her the instant before the summons came, withdrawing in spirit as well as in body, and she could only suppose that he was afraid of becoming involved. There had been no pretense on his part about wanting her; some things could not be simulated. But if he suspected her deeper feelings, if he had any inkling of how much she had missed him, how much she had fallen under his spell, then he would probably run as fast as he could in the opposite direction.

Which was funny, she told herself, combing through her hair with unsteady fingers. Really laughable, when only moments ago he was accusing her of running from him.

The door opened and Reade stood there staring at her. "My God, Bliss, are you all right? Martha said your sister-in-law needed you, but I didn't think . . . I mean, is everything all right?"

That he had missed nothing of her dishevelment was obvious. Did he think, for goodness' sake, that she had been frantically boiling water for some emergency? She stifled a hysterical desire to laugh. "It's nothing to worry about, Reade," she told him. "I came over because Leigh wasn't feeling up to par, and while I was here I thought I'd hang some curtains for her. I'm sorry I forgot our date."

His expression, something between hurt and indignation, told her that she would have a lot of making up to do. So when he said that they still had time to meet the agent, she felt obliged to go along, especially as James was standing there taking it all in. His eyes were as cool and shuttered as if he had not been making the wildest sort of love to her only moments ago. His heart might be beating as slowly and as steadily as a clock at the moment, but it had been racing against hers, leading her breathlessly to heights that left her dizzy.

Holding her coat for her moments later, James eyed the dark green fleece. "Looks new. Whatever happened to the suede one? I rather fancied it."

Bliss turned her gaze around in surprise, not missing the look of open curiosity on Reade's face. "I lost my taste for it," she said shortly.

There was a flash of wicked amusement that was gone almost as quickly as it had come, and then James said he would tell Leigh that she had had to go. "I'll stay until Benji comes home," he assured her. "Thanks for dropping by."

Halfway to Croydon, Bliss wondered what on earth she was doing looking at a house with a man she would never marry but didn't know how to tell him so. How had she allowed herself to drift into such a position? Why had she? She had not missed the look on James's face when Reade told him that they had a date to go look at a house. It had been surprise for just an instant, and then it had been replaced with something akin to contempt, an expression she had not seen on his face since before that weekend in Yorkshire. His voice when he had thanked her for dropping by had been sarcastic, although she doubted if Reade had noticed.

She hated the house. Reade and the agent who had met them there talked enthusiastically about rates and easy commuting and new piping. Bliss sat on a window seat beside a dingy window that looked out on the blank wall of the building next door. There was one struggling ailanthus tree, its thick, stubby branches and twigs moving gracelessly to the wind that channeled between the buildings. She knew she could never live in such a house, nor could she ever marry Reade. The sooner she told him and ended this pathetic charade, the better it would be for both of them.

On the way back for his three o'clock appointment, Reade told her he would have to go to Madrid for at least a week. If she wanted the Croydon house, he would make the call before he left. Now was the time to tell him, only she didn't know how to say it. In the end, she lost her courage and told him only that she didn't really want the house.

"Yes, well, I thought we'd rather like to find something closer to my folks, anyway. But a bloke told me about this one and the terms were good. Oh, well . . . we'll try again when I get back, hmmm?"

The next morning Morton announced plans to spend the day going over a new advertising plan with Adela. "We'll be at her flat if anything comes up, so don't worry if I'm late."

"Who's chaperoning?"

"Don't be impertinent, Miss Bliss," her cousin cracked. "I've managed to avoid being caught since before you were born . . . since *long* before you were born," he added ruefully. "And a Sunday morning alone with a business partner isn't going to compromise me all that much." An odd expression crossed his face as he glanced at her, but it was gone before she could be certain she had even seen it. When she spoke, it was to say, "I like her. Adela, I mean. She may be just a tad outspoken, but that beats obsequiousness any day, in my book. You have to admit, she's awfully well preserved."

"There speaks a twenty-year-old," Morton retorted with a swat at her. "I'll have you know, my brash young maid, that Adela's two years younger than I am and I certainly don't consider myself over the hill."

Bliss had been teasing and they both knew it. Whenever she paid the older woman a compliment, Morton made some derisive comment, but just let her say something slightly derogatory about Adela and he was quick to come to her defense. It occurred to Bliss not for the first time that she might be the only thing standing in the way of their getting together permanently. Then, too, now that Benji no longer lived here, perhaps she should consider setting up somewhere on her own. There was Martha, of course, but all the same . . .

She decided to run over and see how Leigh was faring, not allowing herself to think that James might do the same. Benji greeted her with the news that his wife had slept solidly through the day yesterday and then lay awake half the night.

"Got to get her clock reset, so if you've nothing better to do, come on in and help me keep her awake for a few more hours."

They discussed names for boys and girls. Bliss and Benji reminisced, sending Leigh into gales of laughter when Bliss told her about the time Benji added a gelatinous mass of tadpoles to the huge aquarium that was a part of the decor in their dining room, only to have them mature and emerge on a night when their parents had been entertaining at dinner the mayor and his wife, the minister, his mother and three visiting missionaries.

Bliss helped Leigh take a sponge bath while Benji went out for Chinese food. Afterward they talked some more, with Leigh propped up in the bed that took up most of the room and Bliss trying not to look as uncomfortable as she felt in the one hard chair. The talk turned naturally to siblings, from the Bonners to the Etchisons. When Leigh began to talk about her own brother, Bliss listened avidly.

"It seems as if he's always been my parents . . . both of them. Mom wasn't a maternal sort and Daddy died when I was seven. James took over as soon as he was through school. Then, when Mom died, he moved us into the house in Belgravia and put me in school. He attended all the Parents' Day things and the Field Days and I never really missed not having regular parents. James has been wonderful to me, even when he was going through that thing with Celine. But when I got old enough to start dating, wow! He clamped down on me with an iron hand! He must have thought no one could care for either of us except for our money, which was silly, because lots of the boys I liked had even more than I did. He sewed everything up as far as I'm concerned until I'm twenty-one. Even now that I'm an old married woman and almost a mother, he doesn't think I have sense enough to come in out of the rain. But he's getting to know Benji better and it's going to be all right." She said that last sentence with such a smug conviction that Bliss couldn't help but be reassured.

But who was Celine? This was the second time she had heard the name and she was dying to ask outright, but didn't dare.

Leigh was going on about the baby and the fact

that Benji hoped to be able to afford a house for them after a few years. "He's determined to make it on his own, especially after that thing at work . . ." She broke off in consternation, searching Bliss's face for a reaction.

"I know about it, Leigh," Bliss told her gently.

"Yes, well, he told James that until he'd paid back every cent we'd just have to skimp along, but that he'd support me . . . us . . . with no help from anyone and would not suffer for a single minute. He'll do it, too. He's enormously strong-minded."

Seeing the glowing sheen in those wide eyes, Bliss wondered if she had ever really known her brother. Could a sister ever see beyond the relationship, or was it just that this tiny slip of a girl had brought out another side of Benji's personality? "I'm glad he married you, Leigh," she said now. "You're awfully good for him."

"Yes, well, he's the man I was meant to marry. We both recognized that right from the first, although James made such a fuss. Of course, James would have done that anyway, after what happened to him." With no prompting she went on to tell Bliss about the woman James had planned to marry. "They had bought a lovely house near Hampstead and were spending weekends doing it up. They had dickered for ages with the agent to get it because it belonged to a couple who had died in Ceylon and the estate was in disarray. But anyway, it all got worked out and Jimmy and Celine were going to move in within the month. I didn't really care for her, but he was so happy and I was too young to have much to say about it."

She paused and leaned over to take a sip from the

lemonade Benji had left. Bliss's impatience was about to overpower her, but then the younger girl resumed. "James had some carpet samples he wanted to try with the paint and he knew Celine was tied up at a meeting. So he ran them out himself and found his fiancée and the agent who had sold him the house in . . . what is it they call it? Flagrante delicto?"

Her head shaking protestingly, Bliss whispered, "Oh, no!"

"Oh, yes! So you see why hs amuses himself with women like that MacMurdle one. She's the same type Celine was, awfully beautiful and hard as nails. Only I don't think James saw it at first in Celine. Men can be so terribly blind," she said with all the aplomb of an eighteen-year-old.

"I should think he'd run hard and fast in the other direction."

"Yes, well, even if he is my brother, I can see that James is the sort who needs women, and he believes there's safety in numbers, obviously. At least he knows he won't be tempted into making another mistake if he sticks to the Rona-Celine type who can look after themselves."

During the drive home later in the day, after staying for a Chinese luncheon that was utterly tasteless as far as she was concerned, Bliss went over Leigh's revelations. Safety in numbers, and she was only one more to add to his defense. What was it he had told her? That she didn't add up? Well, it was pretty obvious to her. Even when she had suspected he was only playing games with her—a bird in the hand, so to speak—she had begun to harbor a secret hope that something more serious might grow out of the awkward beginning. He didn't try to hide the fact that he wanted her, but that wasn't enough. To be offered lust when one craved love was as searing to the spirit as a killing frost. If she knew what was good for her, she would take care not be expose herself to any more treatment of that sort.

Chapter Seven

On a day in mid-December when winter took a holiday, Bliss put on her crepe-soled boots, a pair of woolen slacks and a warm anorak and set out after breakfast to walk until she was too tired to think anymore. For days now, and for endless, aching nights, she had known she was irrevocably in love with James Etchison. This was no mere infatuation, based on teasing antagonism and physical attraction; she loved the man, loved his strength and his tenderness, loved the light of humor that struck his eyes, turning silver to gold. And she loved—oh, yes, she might as well admit it—Bliss loved the way he made her feel. All rational thought was abandoned when he held her in his arms.

There had been a few other men on the fringes of her life even before Reade. She was not bad-looking, even though she was no raving beauty like Rona. Her face was passable, she told herself with

honest disregard of her unique blend of features that
added up to more than mere prettiness. The men
who took her out were all attractive and intelligent,
so why had none of them been able to move her to
the point where she lost herself to an overwhelming
wave of pure passion?

With no answers forthcoming, she paced along
under an incredibly blue sky, unconscious of the
children swatting balls and of the pigeons taking
advantage of the rare day to beg a morsel from park
visitors. Perhaps for the first time in her life, she was
totally unconscious of the loveliness of Kensington
Gardens.

She was unable to reach any conclusions during
her outing, but at least she arrived home flushed and
invigorated, and that was something. The mopes
were gone and she felt capable of accomplishing
what had to be done.

As if on cue, Reade's car was pulled up outside
the house, and she swerved to the front instead of
going in through the garden entrance, searching in
her mind for the most painless way to say what had
to be said. In the end, she went out to lunch with
him, to a small pub where her slacks and boots
wouldn't be out of place. There she told him as
gently as she knew how to that she couldn't marry
him, that she didn't intend to marry anyone and that
there was no use trying to get her to change her
mind.

"It's Etchison, isn't it?" he accused, after arguing
with her until she refused to speak to him again.

She remained silent. But something, perhaps the
guilty start at the mention of James's name, gave her
away. When Reade said bitterly that he had known
it ever since she had returned from that weekend in

the country with him, she looked up in shocked dismay. "How did you know about that?"

"The same way half the town knows," he flung at her, signaling for the check. "Don't tell me you thought your little idyll was a secret, for God's sake! I thought if I continued to see you it might take the curse off the worst of the gossip, but if you don't care about your reputation, then why should I?"

Stunned, she demanded to know if that was the only reason he had asked her to marry him, and he had the grace to look ashamed. "I love you, Bliss. I figured nothing happened that weekend, in spite of all the gossip, and soon enough the talk would die down. It has already, really, all but the occasional crack when Etchison shows up somewhere with another of his women on his arm." He cut her a look to see how she was taking it, but her face, she sincerely hoped, reflected nothing of the pain inside her. Perhaps she had underestimated Reade, after all, if he had been man enough to stick by her in spite of all the gossip, for he was a conservative creature and it couldn't have been pleasant.

On the other hand, it made less than a hero out of James, who had subjected her to such a thing and then left her strictly alone.

The ride home was completed in silence, and Bliss was glad. She had said all she could to Reade and it would be best if they cut their losses. Next time maybe he could find someone who wouldn't subject him to such an embarrassment. Now that she thought of it, there had been dozens of clues: the way her friends stopped talking suddenly whenever she approached and then chatted her up so brightly, the odd innuendoes of some of the sales staff at the shop and the way she had caught even Benji eyeing her when she had first returned.

No wonder James had been avoiding her! She must be a real embarrassment to him—in public, at least. He had seemed to enjoy her company well enough at Leigh's flat the other day, she thought with a sudden feeling of warmth, though he had yielded her to Reade readily enough.

Oh, bother! She might just as well be back at St. Elizabeth's with a fifteen-year-old's crush on the music master. She had been teased then and she was being gossiped about now, and neither was fatal.

"I don't guess I'll be calling around anymore. I'm sorry, Bliss. I guess we just weren't right for each other, after all," Reade told her, not quite meeting her eye as he held the door for her.

She felt a deep debt to him and she started to say something conciliatory but then stopped herself. Let it end. There was nothing real between the two of them and they both knew it. Reade was probably glad to be rid of a girl who was this week's scandal, whether she knew it or not.

Before she went up to bed, Morton called her into his study to tell her that James had invited them to dinner on Wednesday evening. "The children as well—a celebration of sorts now that Leigh's back on her feet."

"I'd rather not go if it's all the same," Bliss returned. "I think I might have a headache on Wednesday. Or perhaps I'll run down to the country to visit an old school friend . . . if I can think of one," she grinned weakly.

"Don't be ridiculous! Of course you'll go!" Morton insisted impatiently, turning back to his whisky and evening paper.

"Morton . . ." Bliss began, calling his attention to where she still lingered in the doorway, "did you know about the . . . the talk? I mean about James and me?"

A frown touched his silvered eyebrows as his eyes slid away from her own. "Tempest in a teacup. All done now and nothing the worse for it. Anyone who knows you would know that nothing happened."

"Why didn't you tell me, then? If it was all so harmless, why did I have to hear it from Reade?"

"Oh, well . . ." He shrugged, and Bliss wondered impatiently why it was that men simply ignored anything they didn't want to face.

"Well, at least you can see why I'd rather not have anything more to do with James. That's reasonable enough, isn't it?"

"Not at all. It will give more fuel for gossipmongers if you start snubbing him now."

Exasperated, Bliss exclaimed, "Well, we haven't exactly been keeping company with each other as it is!"

"No, but would you have James himself wonder why you refuse a perfectly innocent family invitation? Especially when he's taking pains to be nice to your brother?"

Warily, she eyed this man who she sometimes suspected had been half in love with her own mother. "Why should I care what James thinks? He's nothing to me."

"Nevertheless, Bliss, you'll attend. I promise you, we'll leave whenever you want to. I don't want to hurt you, child, but it's best if you go along with things right from the first, work it out of your system. Believe me, it's less painful in the long run, because there's no way you can avoid contact with him, considering the various connections. You're related by marriage now, and before you know it, you'll be related by a tiny, red-faced, squalling mite that's half Bonner, half Etchison. You'd better get this thing worked out so that when the time comes, you can handle it like a trouper."

With a wounded cry, she rushed across the room and flung herself on him. "Oh, Morton, what am I going to do? I can no more work this out of my system than I can . . . than I can have brown eyes!" She laughed and caught her breath on a sob as his hands moved compassionately on her shoulders.

"The hurt eases after a while, darling, and you'll find you can live with it. You're young . . . younger than I was, so you have a good chance of a complete remission. At any rate, there's nothing to do except put one foot in front of the other and get yourself through the next day, the next week; and pretty soon, it will be months. It doesn't help to avoid him, love. You only spend your time thinking of what it is you're avoiding." He held her tightly, and when she had gained some control again, he kissed her lightly on the mouth and put her from him.

Then, in a brisker tone of voice, he said, "Guess who I had lunch with today."

"The tooth fairy?" Bliss gurgled, loving this man who had used the same strategy with her when she was a miserable adolescent.

He grimaced. "Not all that far off, young lady. Rona MacMurdle; and if all goes as we hope, the MacMurdles will be better to us than any tooth fairy, by a long shot. Put a fashion line under the pillow and come up with a bundle of American dollars."

"Gad, Morton, you're horrible! Materialistic to

the core!" She eased herself into a more comfortable position and surreptitiously wiped her eyes as he went on to tell her about the outfit Rona had been wearing. Morton's thoughts were never too far from fashion these days, naturally enough, and she thought she must be a sore disappointment to him, as she found the subject utterly boring.

"Aren't you afraid word will filter back to Adela?" she teased.

"Aren't you afraid I'll turn you over my knee for impertinence?" he came back. "Oh, we both know I'll be shackled to that dear managing lady one of these days when I'm no longer strong enough to hold out. But let me dream a bit first, hmmm?"

I'm all for dreams, she heard her heart whisper, but it looks as if you and I are going to have to wake up any day now, because your dream and mine have other ideas.

On Wednesday, Bliss lathered her hair and rinsed it thoroughly and, wrapping a towel around her head, went into Morton's study to dry it by the fire as she considered the coming evening. Since the last time she had seen James, she had learned something about him from his sister, and that knowledge gave her an uneasy feeling, although she could not quite put her finger on the reason.

She plodded back upstairs, her hand trailing along the graceful mahogany baluster, and stood before her closet with unseeing eyes, her mind wandering somewhere between James's past and her own future. As she reached out for a simple gown of woolen crochet in a wood-violet color that flattered her own creamy complexion and chestnut hair, her hand froze. Of course!

James and his Celine had been in the process of readying a house when she succumbed to another man. Bliss herself had been ready to look at a house with Reade when she had made a fool of herself by responding to James. In his eyes, then, she would be no better than his Celine. He couldn't know, not that it would matter to him, that she had broken off her engagement to Reade after that. A little late for honesty, she thought with a bitter smile.

By the time Morton called her for the second time, Bliss had sealed off the past, and now she surveyed herself in the mirror and decided she could hold her head up tonight as far as looks were concerned. The violet dress, its smoky tones rendering her skin almost translucent, brought out the small-scale voluptuousness of her figure and she noticed that the dress fit her rather more loosely than the last time she had worn it. The loss of even a few pounds showed on her, chiefly in her neck, which now looked too fragile to support the thick, waving mass of her hair, and in her face, where new shadows revealed a maturity that was echoed in her eyes.

A necklace of cairngorms set in antique silver completed the outfit and she caught up the fur jacket Morton had given her on her last birthday and hurried down the stairs. It seemed odd not to see Benji; she missed him since he had married. But then, what ever remained the same? Morton, looking suave and debonair in his navy and white evening togs, planted a kiss on her cheek and held her wrap for her and they chatted inconsequentially on the short drive to James's home.

Bliss had never been there before, and she felt her spurious poise begin to ebb away as they pulled up before a tall creamy stucco residence with black shutters and door, a discreet touch of wrought iron and a marvelous fanlight over the door. They were met at the door by James himself, looking unfairly attractive in a classically styled tuxedo. He led them across a marble-floored foyer into one of the most charming rooms Bliss had ever seen.

The woman in her appreciated the warm comfort of the squashy velvet cushions and enormous wing chairs, with functional-sized tables of several periods placed handy for books, ashtrays and tea things. At the same time the decorator in her was thrilled by the clever blend of muted colors and neutrals that accented the priceless Chinese rugs and impressionist paintings. There were several generous, informal arrangements of flowers which gave the room a final embellishment, and Bliss released a sigh of pure appreciation.

Leigh and Benji were already there and Benji stood and crossed the room to kiss her cheek. It occurred to Bliss that less than three months ago, he would have settled for waving a finger at her, if he had noticed her at all. She took a seat beside Leigh, who wore her new maturity as she would have worn a diamond tiara—proudly, but somewhat self-consciously. The younger girl was full of their plans for the flat, plans Bliss thought a bit ambitious considering that it was only two and a half rooms.

"There's no hurry," James said, pouring Bliss the Madeira she requested and handing Morton something stronger. "You may well find it too small after the baby comes, so I wouldn't advise you to put too much effort into renovating it now."

Benji protested and they argued amicably until James's man, who was named Balderdam, summoned them to dinner. It was as they were filing into the perfectly proportioned dining room that the doorbell pealed and Balderdam admitted Rona Mac-Murdle in a swirl of cold air and expensive perfume.

"Darling, I was in the neighborhood and I thought . . . but you're entertaining! Oh, don't mind me, I'll just skip out and you won't even know I've been here," she exclaimed with a charming moue. She hovered, her sable half off her shoulders, and looked provocatively apologetic, and James responded as Bliss knew he would.

"Not at all, Rona. I'm delighted to see you. You must join us."

Bliss tried and failed to interpret his very correct tone. He had little choice under the circumstances. All the same, did he have to look quite so delighted to see her?

Rona hooked a silk-clad arm through James's and another through Morton's, leaving Bliss to follow along with Leigh and Benji. ·

It was a mark of Balderdam's efficiency that by the time they entered the dining room, there was already another setting of Minton and Waterford. As the elderly man discreetly placed the silver, James ushered Rona into the seat at his left, handing Bliss into the one on his right. Bliss told herself that at least she had been given preferential placement, but it was small comfort, for Rona, her sparkling mind jumping from topic to topic, held forth to the exclusion of all others. The evening subtly changed flavor, going from a small, intimate family dinner to a social gathering where Rona skillfully took to herself the role of hostess.

After a dinner that began with stuffed artichokes and ended with Stilton and a pale, dry sherry, James led them from the room. When Bliss paused to admire an especially fine chinoiserie cabinet, James told her that he also had a Korean Imperial Palace chest of burled elm that dated from the eighteenth century and offered to show it to her.

Rona turned as if to follow them, but Morton intervened skillfully and then James was leading Bliss up the curved stairway, his hand touching her arm lightly as he commented on various pieces of furniture. He was as impersonal as any tour guide. All the same, Bliss couldn't keep her pulse from dancing as she stole a glance at his imposing profile.

James nodded to several open doors, and Bliss caught a glimpse of soft colors and handsome textures. Then he was ushering her into a large, airy room done in tobacco brown and white with touches of celadon, and she knew it was his own.

"The chest," he murmured, leading her unresisting form across the thick carpet to the elegant commode with its brass butterfly accents.

Neither of them gave it more than a cursory glance. James's hands had fallen to his sides but his eyes held Bliss as if by magnetic force. When she murmured that it was lovely, he ignored her words as if she had not spoken. "You look like the first violet of the season in that thing, all brave and defenseless at the same time."

"Don't," she whispered, unable to escape the silver seine of his eyes.

"Are you embarrassed at being in my bedroom?"

"No, of course not." She played cool. "One normally sees bedrooms in a tour of the house."

"You know very well what I mean, so don't go all prickly and defensive on me," he taunted, leaning back against the small, delicate cabinet as if his large frame were not in danger of crushing its ancient, fragile wood.

"I think we'd better join the others." She stepped back, tugging at the hand he had taken. He straightened and propelled her into his arms as she sighed fatalistically, "Oh, James, not again!"

"You've been waiting for this moment almost as much as I have," he told her. "Look . . ." He touched the place at the base of her throat where her pulse beat frantically. When his lips touched her temple, her eyes, and then slipped down to her mouth, twisting gently to crumple her lips beneath his own, she moved involuntarily to align her body to his, letting her arms slip up his shoulders and around his neck. She lost all sense of reason, knowing only the compelling directives of her own body as his mouth worked over hers, teasing, tantalizing, probing for acceptance into the depths of its warm moisture. She found herself lying across his bed, and something hard and pagan flowered inside her as she gave herself up to the dangerous excitement of the moment, meeting passion with passion as James's warm hands explored and caressed her with a tense gentleness.

As he triggered switch after switch, turning her deliberately into a mass of quivering nerve endings, she fought against saying the words that hovered on her tongue, words that would put her completely at his mercy. When the sound of voices reached the dim recesses of her mind, she was almost glad, as if someone had tossed her a lifeline just as she was about to resign herself to the rapture of the deep.

"Oh, God," James groaned against the overheated skin of her throat. "Bliss, you must . . ."

Rona called from the other side of the door. James must have closed it after them and she hadn't even known it. Now she heard with faint disbelief the rattling of the knob.

"James! Are you in there? The door's locked!"

"Pull yourself together, darling," James murmured softly, his smile a mere twisting of that sensual mouth beneath eyes that were still black with passion. "You look as if you've been thoroughly made love to."

"I have," she replied shakily, smoothing her hair and adjusting the bodice of her gown where James's questing hands had pulled it aside. Her breasts still ached for the touch of his fingers and the feel of his mouth.

"Not yet, you haven't, but you will, you will," he promised, crossing the floor to open the door to Rona, who stood there impatiently tapping her foot in the hallway.

"The latch is tricky," he told her, quite his usual urbane self by now. "It wasn't locked . . . see? I was showing Bliss the chest over there, since she's interested in interior decoration."

"Oh, is that what she's interested in?" Rona said thinly, eyeing the other girl closely through narrowed lids.

"I . . . I've been redoing Morton's house bit by bit," Bliss explained, glancing at the bed to see if she had removed the wrinkles, "but for all his antiques, he doesn't have anything like this."

"Frankly, old furniture is old furniture, no matter what you call it. Mother and Father have collected half the junk in Bucks County and you can't walk through their place without endangering life and limb. There are far more fascinating things in life than woodworm and dry rot as far as I'm concerned."

James urged them out and closed the door after him, and Rona got in one more gibe: "Be careful it doesn't catch, dear. It'd be a shame to find yourself locked out of your own bedroom."

Downstairs again, Bliss excused herself and went to find the powder room that Leigh had pointed out to her. She badly needed time to gather herself together. Once in the seclusion of the elegant little room, she seated herself before a French mirror and clasped her pale cheeks with shaking hands. God, what was she thinking about to fall into his arms like an overripe plum? There was no future in it. Hadn't Leigh as much as said that he would never fall in love, never marry? There was nothing between her and James except for a certain elementary antagonism and a whale of a physical attraction, certainly nothing on which to base a more permanent relationship.

Oh, quit fooling yourself, you silly mooncalf! You're simply trying to rationalize the fact that you're in love with a lost cause! She stared into her own eyes, seeing the remnants of a passion that had shaken her through and through, and the beginning of the misery that would take its place. When the door opened behind her and another image appeared in the oval glass beside her, she tried on a smile that failed completely.

She might as well not have made the effort.

"Just what are you trying to pull, Bliss Bonner?" Rona demanded, her bone-thin figure in pale blue silk gleaming against the dark linenfold carving behind her.

"I'm trying to pull this hair of mine back into

141

place long enough to anchor it," Bliss answered facetiously, fingering the hairpins that held her chignon in place.

"You know what I mean! Seeing the house, indeed! You could hardly wait to get him into his bedroom, could you? What's the matter, didn't you play your cards right that weekend you spent with him in Yorkshire? And what did your fiancé think about your running off across country with another man for a little fun and games?"

"Don't be crude, Rona," Bliss said quietly, getting to her feet and attempting to pass the older woman.

"Crude, is it? I'm not the one who's crude enough to attempt to trap a man by the oldest trick in the book! And while she's engaged to someone else, at that! There's a name for your sort, but if you don't want to hear it, I'd advise you not to do any eavesdropping on your friends. You've given them all something to serve up with tea and crumpets."

"There's only one person who'd have repeated that affair, Rona, and I can't think why you find it necessary to discredit me. Didn't it occur to you that you were hurting James, as well?"

"Don't be stupid! Hurting James? Any man will take what's offered up to him on a platter and any fool knows it, too, so don't give me that song and dance! The old double standard is still on the books, in spite of women's lib. You can't blame James for taking what's offered, especially as your own fiancé doesn't seem to care one way or another."

Bliss took a deep breath and felt behind her for the steadiness of the wall. "Not that it's any of your business, but Reade and I are not, nor have we ever been, engaged," she said with quiet dignity.

"Oh?" Rona sneered. "If you say so, but it looks to me as if the two of you came unglued just after that little fling with James up in the hills. Could it be that you were dumped? Maybe old Reade isn't the forgiving clod you took him for, hmmm?"

"You'll believe what you want to believe and it really doesn't matter to me, Rona," Bliss said impassively, moving toward the door with a firmness of purpose that made the other woman step aside.

"Yes, I will, as a matter of fact, but, Bliss—just so there's no misunderstanding between us—don't let it happen again. I overlooked it the first time because . . . well, James and I hadn't made our plans official . . . then." Her opaque eyes, so like painted porcelain, stared at Bliss superciliously, and Bliss lifted her head and walked out the door, not daring to release the breath she had caught and held until she stood alone on the cold, formal squares of marble in the foyer.

Did she believe Rona? Could she believe anything that viper said? Was there an engagement, or even an understanding between James and Rona?

No, certainly not! James would have told her, and besides, he wouldn't have acted as he had upstairs with his own fiancée under his roof—would he?

Remembering what Leigh had said about her brother and the way he had reacted to the deep hurt he had been dealt by a woman, it was not possible to know how he would act, she admitted miserably. And for her own self-preservation, she couldn't afford to lose sight of that fact.

Chapter Eight

Christmas came and brought with it a gray, wet snow that melted as it fell, making travel hazardous as well as unpleasant. Morton had invited several people over to dinner on Boxing Day, including James and Rona, Adela and the young Bonners. When Bliss tackled him about his guest list, he refuted her arguments easily. Whom could he have left off? James was a family as well as a business connection, and Rona was a friend as well as a business connection, a guest in their country without the comfort of her own family about her.

Bliss swallowed her rude comments about that particular item and reminded herself that it *was* Morton's home, after all, and if it came down to it, she was only a guest herself. At least Reade was not included, which might make it possible for her to slip off after dinner and allow Adela to take over the reins as hostess.

Leigh was looking radiant in a totally unnecessary maternity outfit and Benji looked as if he could eat her with a spoon. Bliss allowed herself a smug, I-told-you-so look at James once during the early evening when Benji directed his wife's hand toward a nonalcoholic drink with a lift of an eyebrow and she only beamed fatuously at him.

Rona had come along with James, of course, and Bliss forced herself to make polite conversation for the few minutes before Adela arrived. Then she took the older woman aside, complimented her sincerely on her smart teak-brown silk suit and explained that she would like to slip away after a while with as little disturbance as possible, and would Adela look after things for Morton in her absence?

She would, and Bliss could see she was pleased to be asked. So far, so good. Now, if she could only keep from speaking her mind to Rona MacMurdle and her heart to James Etchison, she might get through the next hour or so with a facade of dignity.

It was all but impossible to keep from following James with her eyes. His dark mohair suit fit with an ease that allowed him to move freely, and yet there was no disguising the lean, well-knit body beneath it. He was the perfect guest, chatting impartially among the others, charming Adela and treating Benji with an easy camaraderie. His eyes rested often on Bliss, but he found no occasion to speak to her other than the murmured greeting when he arrived.

Dinner went off without a hitch, for Bliss had spent long hours with Martha in the kitchen, preparing oyster stuffing for the smoked turkey and making a salad of tiny green peas, scallions, water chestnuts and boiled eggs in a creamy dressing. Now, with strawberry cake to follow, and even the blasé Adela remarking on the tomato bisque served with tiny shrimp floating on paper-thin slices of cucumber, Bliss relaxed the tight control she had maintained over herself and sat back with a feeling of self-congratulation. If she could carry off an evening of watching James and Rona together, she could handle almost anything.

Across the disarray of the table, Bliss caught Adela's eye and nodded imperceptibly. They all arose and wandered out, still talking in small groups. Leigh and Benji were discussing their favorite topic, while Rona and Adela continued sniping at each other in a desultory manner. Morton and James were talking about something in an undertone, and Bliss watched them curiously as they paused in the door, still talking earnestly.

She had planned to slip away now, but with James and Morton still standing in the doorway, her leaving might be a little conspicuous, especially as James, still speaking to Morton, was allowing his glance to move over her in a disconcerting way. Trying to look busy with the candles in the dining room while she waited for them to move on, she wondered self-consciously if he could tell the care she had taken with her appearance tonight. The dress was new, a soft, flowing design of mingled shades of heather, rose and silvery green. She had done her hair in a different style, coiling it around on top of her head for height and allowing the tendrils to curl softly about her face. Nothing to compare with Rona's elegance, surely, but all the same, she thought she looked rather nice.

When Morton clapped James on the shoulder and turned to go into the drawing room, she waited impatiently for James to follow him, but instead, the younger man turned toward where she tarried in the dining room.

"Not finished in here yet?"

"Just checking to be sure the candles didn't drip on the linen," she prevaricated.

He took her arm and, switching out the light behind them, urged her into Morton's study across the hall and closed the door firmly. "I didn't notice any mistletoe among your handsome decorations," he commented, seeming to have dropped the urgency now that they were alone.

"Sorry. Maybe next year." Bliss instinctively crossed her arms defensively. "We'd better return to the others before they start to wonder what happened to us."

"Who'll wonder?"

She shrugged and avoided his intense gaze. Rona, she could have told him, and she could well do without a repeat of the last episode. "What did you want, James?"

"Perhaps I was curious why Reade Johnston isn't here tonight?" he suggested.

"We . . . we haven't been seeing each other lately."

"Would it have anything to do with that weekend we spent together?" he ventured.

Bliss glared up at him. "I wish everyone would stop referring to it that way! We didn't spend it together, at least not in that sense, and you know it!"

"I take it you've finally heard about the talk. I'm sorry, Bliss. I wouldn't have had that happen for the world."

She eyed him doubtfully. "Wouldn't you? It occurs to me that it might be a fine way to revenge yourself against the Bonner family, to do to Benji's sister what he did to yours." Then the possible connotation of her words struck her and she blushed hotly. "I mean my reputation," she hastened to add, "the scandal and all."

His reaction shook her thoroughly. A sudden grayness came over his harsh features, but when he spoke, his voice was almost totally under control. "I'm sorry if you thought that of me, Bliss. I had hoped you knew me better." He shrugged and turned away. "So Johnston dropped you because we spent an illicit weekend. I suppose I should say I'm sorry—not that I believe you really loved him. Still, I know how one's pride can suffer in a case like that, having once been on the receiving end myself. If it would help, I'd be glad to speak to him, to assure him that his would-be bride is still entitled to her white wedding gown . . . at least as far as I'm concerned."

Indignation stung her and she spat out her words: "You're hateful! I wish you'd just forget the whole thing, forget we ever met, for that matter! I don't think we have anything more to say to each other, so, if you don't mind, I'll return to the others before your lady friend comes looking for you again!"

"One gathers that you aren't too fond of Rona MacMurdle. I wonder . . . is it on Morton's account, or my own? I understand he's been seeing something of her off and on, between the times when she's out with me."

"It must be nice to be so in demand!" she snapped, despising herself for such petty remarks. "You're both welcome to her as far as I'm concerned, and she to you, although I think Morton deserves better."

He laughed aloud at that, reducing Bliss to impotent fury, and she brushed past him with a militant sparkle in her eye, only to be caught easily and hauled up against his pristine shirtfront.

"Mistletoe or not, I think I deserve greetings of the season, don't you?" he asked softly, proceeding to take what he wanted from her stubbornly resistant lips. "Open your mouth, you little firebrand," he muttered against the corner of her lips, reaching up to catch her chin between thumb and forefinger. "Now kiss me . . . kiss me as if you meant it and I might allow you to return to the others."

"Go to hell!" Bliss raged against his warm, marauding mouth, and he took advantage of her response to plunder the sweet depths of her, forming her reluctant body to his until she caught fire from his own arousal and yielded helplessly.

Only when she was at the point of utter helplessness, arching herself to him involuntarily, her hands moving restlessly up his lean, muscular sides beneath his jacket, did he put her from him, grinning lazily down into her bemused face.

"I need your help this next week or so, Bliss."

"You what?" she asked, bewildered.

"I've a house near Hampstead that's recently been vacated. It's small enough not to be unwieldy, but large enough for a growing family, with large enough grounds and within easy commuting distance. I want to look it over with you, and if you agree, we'll offer it to Leigh and Benji."

Her mind had to race to catch up with his meaning, having come from a state of complete inertia brought about by his lovemaking, and she stared up at him, her soft, unfocused eyes the color of ripe acorns. "Have you told them about it?"

"No, of course not. I wouldn't want to get their hopes up in case we decided it wasn't just the thing."

"But why do you need me? Surely you're capable of deciding on your own."

"I need a woman's viewpoint. You seem to have a feel for that sort of thing. So I thought you'd be the ideal one to say if it will be too much for Leigh or easy enough for her to manage. Morton and I agree that Benji's been working hard enough lately to have earned a small increase. That, plus what they can save on the flat, will be enough to support the place, I believe. Of course, both of them have resources they're not presently using, but that will come later. At any rate, what do you say? Shall I pick you up tomorrow and we'll see the place and then discuss it over dinner somewhere?"

"Whoa! You're going too fast for me," she stalled, moving further away so that she could think more clearly. The spell of that magnetically attractive body and those steely eyes was enough to undo her completely, and she needed all her wits about her to cope with this newest development, especially with Rona in the next room, a Rona who might or might not be his fiancée. She was tempted to ask him about it outright, but she lacked the courage, fearing his anger—or his answer.

It was agreed that he would pick her up at ten-thirty; that would give them time enough to pick up the keys from the agent and poke around the grounds as well as going through the house. When they returned to the others, Morton had turned on the stereo and Leigh and Benji were dancing, with Benji holding his small wife with an exaggerated care that brought a sting to Bliss's eyes. And then Rona appeared to lead James out onto the floor, and Bliss slipped away into the kitchen to help Martha clear away, leaving Morton and Adela arguing good-naturedly.

In spite of her own decision to leave them to it, Bliss found herself carrying in the tray of mulled cider and cheese biscuits. After half an hour or so, Benji pulled Leigh to her feet, making their excuses to leave. "Have to tuck her in, you know. She's sleeping for two these days."

Bliss saw them off and returned to hear Morton asking James if he had mentioned the house yet.

"Yes, Bliss and I are seeing it tomorrow. If it's feasible, I'll have cleaners and carpenters in before the New Year and we'll see how fast we can get it shaped up."

"Oh, what house is this?" Rona asked brightly. When Morton proceeded to enlighten her, she exclaimed that she had always wanted to see that area. "I understand there are some fabulous places out in that direction . . . Hampstead Heath and such."

With a certain fatalism, Bliss heard her insinuate herself into the proposed outing and there was not a thing she could do about it. There was no reason why Rona shouldn't be allowed to accompany them; all the same, Bliss could have wept!

The party broke up shortly after that, with Morton driving Adela home and James ushering Rona out into the frosted night air. "Ten-thirty," he

151

reminded Bliss at the door. She offered him a rather wan smile and closed the door after them.

When morning came, bringing with it an unseasonable thaw, Bliss dressed slowly in a dark green knit two-piece dress, her brown suede boots and an amber print scarf. She tried to think of an excuse for not going. As soon as she thought of one, she immediately rationalized it away, so that by the time the doorbell sounded, she was thoroughly out of sorts.

"Mind you get back here at a reasonable hour, now," Martha scolded. "Don't trust this thaw one bit, and it wouldn't surprise me if we didn't have more snow by midnight."

"I'll have her back before my coach turns into a pumpkin, Martha, never fear," James assured the plump housekeeper as he ushered Bliss out to the waiting car. This time, instead of the black Maserati, he was driving a dark gray Jensen, and Rona was firmly ensconced in the front seat.

They greeted each other warily, each knowing the other wished her in perdition, and James slid under the wheel and tooled away. They circled west of Regent's Park and then took the A41 northward, with James chatting easily to both of them. Before they had gone halfway, Rona had picked up the conversational ball and was playing strictly in her own court, leaving Bliss to stare out the window at the winter-sere scenery.

By the time they turned off onto a country road, and again into a poorly kept driveway, the sky had taken on a sickly gray look. A row of skeletal trees etched darkly against that sky announced the presence of the modest-sized but beautifully designed house which James told them was called Mallows. Any mallows in the overgrown garden today, though, were hardly in evidence.

"Gad, how dismal," Rona snorted, huddling deeper in her seat as James pocketed the key and turned halfway around.

"What do you think, Bliss? Needs lots of work, of course, but they're young and energetic."

"This isn't the sort of weather to show it up to the best advantage, of course, but did you notice how the windows seem to give it expression? Sort of a sleepy smile? With a coat of paint and the mullion repaired . . . and that must be clematis on the trellis. It will be perfect by the time . . ."

He nodded and opened the door, helping Bliss out before going around to the other side to Rona.

"It'll be cold as a tomb." Rona shivered. "I hope you're not planning to stay more than a few minutes. Even after Bucks County, I'm not used to your winters here . . . so awfully damp!"

James assured her that if she got too chilled, she could return to the car and switch on the heater. Instead of glaring at James, she shot Bliss a look of pure dislike.

The pale, watery light was not kind to a house that had been emptied of a recent tenant. The hollow echo of their footsteps seemed to drop the temperature several degrees, but Bliss fell behind the other two and made an effort to visualize a warm fire on the hearth and a scattering of assorted cheerful rugs, with a creeper and a toddler and perhaps a large, shaggy dog. There would be a comfortable untidyness about the place—toys, nappies drying on the fire screen, a pipe rack with a few shreds of tobacco and a magazine folded open to an unfinished article, awaiting the time when both babies were asleep and two people could relax in warm companionship.

She broke off, aghast at the direction her unruly thoughts had taken. Benji didn't smoke a pipe, although she had seen one in James's bedroom. As far as she knew, Leigh didn't read much, preferring the telly or a bit of music.

"Bliss? Discouraged already?" James asked ruefully from the doorway. The light was behind him, outlining his bulky frame in the familiar sheepskin jacket and creating a nimbus around his dark head with its premature silver.

"Only daydreaming," she admitted. "Furnishing the room with babies, rugs, dogs and assorted litter. What's the upstairs like?"

They trooped up, with Rona careful to stay beside James. When Bliss lingered too long in a small room that would catch the morning sun, envisioning rabbit-print curtains and a matching panel of paper in one end, it was Rona who pushed her along.

"I'm freezing! Come on, Bliss, let's go! There's certainly nothing more to see here, unless you plan to check the basement for termites. God, just look at that sky! It's practically snagging on the treetops!"

They left, with Bliss peering behind to try to picture the garden as it might look in the springtime. If they did decide to give it to the youngsters—they! If James decided, then she would just have to manage to get out here and put in a few hours getting the grounds ready for springtime. Bulbs would have to go in soon and there was a good bit of pruning to be done. Perhaps she could borrow Mr. Timmons, who did the heavy work in Morton's neighborhood.

It was snowing before they reached the A40 intersection. When Rona asked about dinner plans, James told her shortly that the first priority was to reach town.

It was a wet snow. In the back seat, Bliss dozed, hearing an occasional whump-whump sound as they passed another vehicle. The air was thick and cottony and by the time they reached town, with its heavier traffic, an odd sort of light was illuminating the sky. Rona had evidently run out of conversation, especially as James seemed intent on his driving. When they turned west to go around Hyde Park in the Mayfair area and eventually pulled up in front of Rona's hotel, she aroused to protest angrily.

"Forgive me if I'm wrong, but didn't you say something about dinner?" She eyed Bliss balefully over the back of the seat as James explained rather impatiently that, considering the weather and the deteriorating driving conditions, he thought it expedient to get everyone safely home, and then her expression turned positively acid.

Before more could be said, James was holding her door. He escorted her to the door of her hotel, where a uniformed doorman tipped a snow-covered hat. From her position in the back seat, Bliss watched what appeared to be an exchange of sharp words, and then Rona reached up and pulled James's head down and kissed him, regardless of the onlookers. Bliss grunted to herself in disgust, folding her arms on her chest. When James returned she was intently observing a lorry, which had no business being there in the first place, trying to negotiate a narrow service alley.

The door beside her opened, letting in a blast of

cold, wet air. "Get into the front," James ordered peremptorily.

"I'm perfectly all right here since we haven't far to go."

Without another word he slammed the door, moving swiftly around the bonnet to slide in under the wheel. They glided away and melded with the stream of slowly moving traffic. Bliss closed her eyes and tried to doze again, realizing moments later that her jaw was clenched and her fists dug into her arms through the fabric of her coat.

They came to the end of Park Lane, but instead of turning toward Kensington, James cut south in the direction of Belgrave Square. Before she could question him they had turned into James's street and once more he was ordering her out of the car. She stepped out under a plane tree, its grotesque branches writhing darkly against the thick, hushed sky, and James said, "Come on now, there's no need to ruin another good coat."

"Why are we stopping here?" she stalled, licking a snowflake from her bottom lip.

James eyed her narrowly, his dark bulk looming coercively against the pale, grayed landscape. "Why court disaster for the sake of another few miles in this mess? You'll be perfectly all right here, I assure you. Balderdam can rustle us up some supper, and then, when it slacks up, I'll take you home, safe and sound."

"And what if it doesn't slack up?" she demanded suspiciously.

"Why, then we'll call Morton and let him know you're all right." He left her no room for argument as he practically pushed her through the door. When they stood dripping on the marble squares, she tried to think of some logical comeback and could find none.

Or perhaps she simply didn't try awfully hard. There was no way she could tell him how very vulnerable she felt with him, but then, for all she knew, he was simply thinking of his expensive fenders. After all, he had been driving a good many miles today, and the last bit under difficult circumstances. All the same, she couldn't hide her doubts, and when he teased her, promising not to seduce her before supper, she felt the color rising to warm her cheeks all too readily.

"You're blushing," he said, touching her face with a forefinger.

"It's the cold . . . the warmth . . . oh, you know what I mean!" she flashed angrily, relinquishing her coat and tugging at the knit top she wore.

"Boots damp? I'm afraid my own slippers would swallow you. But if you don't mind skipping about on the carpet in your stocking feet, we'll leave them in the airing closet to dry slowly."

"That won't be necessary," she said repressively. "I'm sure the weather will clear up in a little while so that you can take me home, of if you'd rather not go out again, I can call Morton and he'll pick me up. In fact, I'll just give him a ring now, if I may?"

"No problem. Go on in to the fire and I'll give him a ring. I'll have to tear Balderdam away from his thriller, anyway, and have him fix us a bite to eat."

Well aware of her cowardly weakness, Bliss did as she was told, dropping down onto a low, down-filled sofa before a real log fire. No electric log for James, at least not in this room. She inhaled the delicious fragrance of applewood as it mingled with the scent of a well-cared-for room.

"Come on, get those boots off," James ordered several minutes later. He reached down to tug at the toe and the brass-trimmed heel.

"Did you reach Morton?" Bliss was forced to lean back and brace herself as James removed first one boot, then the other, managing to expose quite an expanse of nylon-clad leg in the process. She tugged her stretchy skirt down over her knees as he sat down beside her.

"Nope. Your housekeeper said he was having dinner with Miss Cadoux and that she would expect you when she saw you, now that she knew you were back in town and in good hands."

Somehow, that news only served to increase Bliss's feeling of uneasiness, but she could think of nothing to say.

They dined well on cream of leek soup and lobster salad, and afterward, back in the living room in front of a softly hissing fire, they shared sections of the *Telegraph* over coffee, commenting on bits of news. From time to time Bliss got up and wandered over to the window, only to be confronted with a solid blanket of snow that gave a peculiar hush to the almost nonexistent traffic outside.

The only sound was the hiss and crackle of the fire on the hearth, and when James got up and announced that it was time for the news, Bliss resented the intrusion. But as he switched on the telly she settled back down, choosing one of the three wing chairs, this one covered in a faded brocade that wore its age extremely well.

During the sports coverage, James got up and poured them both a drink. Rather than argue, Bliss accepted the small whisky, nursing it without tasting it while the announcer went on to regale his audience with the latest scandal concerning a prominent barrister, a well-known sculptor and a name familiar to all theatergoers.

"Afraid I'm attempting to get you drunk so that I can have my way with you, as the phrase goes?" James teased, nodding at her untouched drink.

"Certainly not!"

"No need to fear for your reputation, you know. That"—he indicated the news commentator, who had gone on to give stock market quotations by now—"will more than fill the slot when our escapade fades out of sight."

"I wasn't worried about the talk. I never really heard it, you know . . . just *of* it. Do you think we might try the road again?" She stood up restlessly after putting the drink down on the table. James stood, too, suddenly seeming far closer to her than could be accounted for by the distance between their two chairs.

"No, we can't, and it was never really that bad, you know. The talk, I mean, not the weather. Only a few speculations in small circles. Neither of us warrants that much interest unless we do something really outrageous, and in this day and time, spending an unauthorized weekend alone is neither here nor there."

Bliss couldn't argue the point. She backed away, only to come up against her chair, and she stammered, "Do . . . do you think the roads are clear enough now?"

"Are you afraid of me, Bliss? You needn't be, you know. I wouldn't hurt you."

"I know that." Her breast rose and fell at a rapidly increasing rate as she became more agitated by his closeness. The mild, urbane voice, the proper solicitude of the perfect host, none of these did a thing to allay her unease. When he offered to show her to her room, she almost bolted.

"Come now, Bliss, Balderdam would be perfectly willing to do the honors. But why should we get the poor old man up and have him struggle back into his coat and shoes when he's relaxing with his feet up, enjoying his third tot of gin? I promise you . . . nothing except a brother-in-law's concern for your comfort. Well, perhaps a chaste handshake, hmmm?"

She couldn't help but respond to his mood with a reluctant grin. In all honesty, everything he said was perfectly reasonable. It was foolish to risk an accident when she was safe and sound in a house with plenty of room, with a relative of sorts . . . very loosely connected or not. Snow tires were all very well, but when the snow was coming down at such a rate that one couldn't see three feet in front of one's nose, why take unnecessary risks?

The room he showed her to was one she had glimpsed and liked the time she had come here before. It was a moderately small room done up in faded rose, moss green and ivory, with fruitwood furniture and a small, tiled electric fireplace.

"The bath is through there," he indicated, "and I think you'll find everything you need short of nightwear, but then I happen to know you're pretty resourceful on that subject. I'll wake you with coffee in the morning."

"Don't bother," she said dryly, resenting the reminder of another time.

He ignored her sarcasm. "Bliss . . . I'm going to kiss you and then I'll go."

Before she could react to his startling announcement, he had drawn her to him, holding her so that he could look down and cover her face with an almost palpable scrutiny. And then he lowered his head and she was ready, her lips parting breathlessly in spite of all her fine resolutions. The kiss went on and on. Inside, she was crying out for it never to end even as she sensed his holding back. He held her away from him then, his eyes shadowed and unreadable, and when she would have moved back into the circle of his arms, he stepped away and said, "If you need me in the night, call out. I'm just next door."

Of that I'm all too painfully aware, Bliss whispered to herself as he closed the door behind him, leaving her standing in her stocking feet on the deep ivory carpet. There was a sort of hushed expectancy in the room after he walked out, and for all it was after midnight, she thought she was going to have an awfully hard time falling asleep.

Chapter Nine

To Bliss's distinct disappointment, when morning came, she was awakened by a soft tap on her door. Then Balderdam called out that breakfast would be ready in ten minutes and that Mr. James had gone to the office but would be back in an hour to take her home.

She was dressed and waiting, struggling to put into proper perspective her lingering feeling of disappointment, when James let himself in the front door. The cold and wet weather came in with him and he peeled off his pigskin gloves, brushed a few flakes of snow from his bare head and grinned broadly at her as he rubbed his hands together briskly.

"Had breakfast? Good! Snow's all but ended now and the streets are in good enough shape."

On the drive home there was none of the comfortable intimacy they had shared the night before. Instead, there was a brisk air of impersonal friendliness that both puzzled and annoyed Bliss. But what else should she expect, for heaven's sake? Just because James had been forced by the weather to share his home with her last night, there was absolutely no reason to think she meant anything more to him than . . . than Benji, for instance. No, not even as much.

"I think the house will do very well, don't you? I'll have the cleaners in and get everything put in first-class condition and we'll leave the redecorating to the happy homeowners."

"That's awfully generous of you, James, especially considering . . . well, you know."

He slanted her a quick look as he negotiated a corner. "You mean because I strongly disapproved of your brother and did everything I could to keep them apart?"

Her fingers curved into her gloved palms. "Yes, I mean that, as well as the other thing . . . at work, I mean."

"When I was younger than Benji, I ran away from school, spent a term bumming around South America before I even let my father know where I was. Most of us have to rebel in one way or another. It takes a jolt of some sort to sever the cord. Benji's rebellion took an unfortunate direction, but luckily it was short-lived. I think Leigh had a lot to do with his . . . reformation. The love of a good woman and all that tripe!" His sarcasm came as such a wrench after the way he had begun that Bliss could only stare at him in anguish.

When she had caught her breath, she spoke without thinking. "And you don't believe in the power of that love, of course." The minute the words left her mouth she could have bitten off her tongue, remembering what had happened to him from believing in just such a commodity.

If it bothered him, he didn't show it. "What about you, Bliss? Have you rebelled yet? Have you cut the cord, or are you just a small satellite of your home background?"

That needed a moment of consideration. "I . . . as a matter of fact, I think the cord was cut for me when I was fourteen. Since then . . ."

"Sorry," James said, obviously meaning it. "I should have thought, but sometimes one says things in jest that . . . but to continue along those lines, would you consider a weekend with a man you didn't love as a breakaway?"

She slowly turned a fiery red as she stared down at the clenched hands in her lap. "I think you've lost your mind! Here, don't miss the turn!"

"I know very well where the turn is, Bliss. I take it your answer is no. On what grounds, I wonder? Protecting your reputation, or protecting your security with Morton? Surely you can't be one of those nonliberated ladies who hold out for the magic ring, can you?"

"I think you're being unusually beastly this morning, even for you. As far as I know, I haven't done anything to make you speak to me like this . . . have I?" She was unable to keep the baffled hurt from her eyes as she stared at his profile, trying to understand his strange mood.

"Will you help me with the house? Go over it once more to see if there are any major renovations to be completed before they can move in, will you? I think it would be a good idea if they make the move as soon as possible so that Leigh can do what she thinks she has to do before she gets too unwieldy."

Bliss was staggered by his restless change of mood. All she could do was nod in agreement. The house, after all, was as important to Benji as it was to Leigh, and Bliss, as his sister, had an interest in it, only she hoped it wouldn't mean her spending too much time in the company of this baffling man. Her nervous system wouldn't bear up under much more of this treatment. Not only did he leave her feeling battered after almost every encounter, but she was beginning to doubt herself in almost every respect.

"Tomorrow's New Year's Eve," he said as he pulled up in front of Morton's residence. "I think the MacMurdles are entertaining, so I expect I'll see you there."

"I didn't even know they were back in town," she said weakly. "Rona didn't mention it yesterday."

"Yes, well, there's a lot Rona doesn't mention," James said dryly.

I can well believe that, Bliss told herself, stepping out into a patch of sunlight as the clouds rolled sluggishly aside to reveal an optimistic-looking sun.

"I'll see you tomorrow night at Josh's, then. New Year's celebrations leave me cold as a rule, but since this is quasi business, I'll be putting in an appearance. You'll be coming with Morton, I suppose."

She allowed him to suppose as much, hurrying inside with no more than a casual wave of her hand. No, she wouldn't be attending the party, not to see Rona parade her claim, however questionable, to James! She would bet even money there was no engagement involved, as she had seen no sign of a ring, and James had let Rona off first last night and kept Bliss on.

But then, perhaps his reason was as obvious as he said—the weather. After all, except for one devastating kiss, he had made no attempt to take advantage of her, and she told herself she was glad of that, at least.

Liar, she whispered to herself. Liar, liar, liar!

Morton came home for lunch and admitted that he had been stranded at Adela's flat last night, which gave rise to a great deal of speculation on Bliss's part. Martha, too, eyed them both with a frankly doubtful expression and Bliss buried her nose in the morning paper to avoid any questions, rude or not. Morton occasionally read through his mail at the table and she usually chided him, but today he seemed too distracted to even notice her own backsliding.

It was as he was leaving again for the shop that he mentioned the MacMurdles' party and told her that he would be taking both her and Adela unless she had another date, and Bliss opted out.

"I really don't feel like partying, Morton, especially not a business party. I suppose you'll decorate it with all the girls from the shop as well as half the press and a selected list of favored clients."

"Business is business, honey, and they're not bad company, at that. Even my models have a private life, and you know you like the others. As for the clients . . ." He shrugged. Some were fine, some not so fine, and the really awful ones wouldn't be asked, those like Bruce Pitmann.

"All right," she sighed. It had been unrealistic to imagine that she would be able to get away with staying home on New Year's Eve. "I suppose once everyone has enough of whatever's flowing to lubricate the conversation, we won't be able to tell ours from any other party."

"Atta girl! Wear the bronze number, hmmm? I

believe we'll do a copy of that for MacHenry, along with the rest of the fall collection, and then next spring . . . good Lord, *this* spring! It slips away, doesn't it?"

In spite of her agreement, Bliss knew she couldn't attend the party. It wasn't as if she would be missed. If this was an example of the usual holiday bash which included Morton's business contacts, there would be more than enough people to fill the gap, two of whom she could well do without seeing. A vision of Rona's flawless face swam before her, and enamel-blue eyes set like jewels in beds of thick, improbably dark lashes. And her smile—the one she lavished on James—that had set her father back a small fortune, according to Sybil, who had naively confided the shocking sum they had spent for braces and capping on their only child.

Well, it had been worth it. Rona was beautiful, a social success, *au fait* with all the proper sports and more than capable of holding her own with James Etchison. Morton had mentioned that James had even allowed her to borrow the Maserati several times, which immediately put her in a different category from herself, Bliss acknowledged ruefully. It was a wonder he could ever trust another woman with his precious sports car. It was a wonder he could ever trust another woman, period.

These days, Martha was full of rheumatism and speculation about Morton and his manageress. She wondered aloud more than once if she would care to stay on and work for a foreigner "if worse came to worst."

Bliss was half convinced it would be the best thing that could happen to both Morton and Adela. She didn't know the older woman particularly well, having seen only the small, dark exterior with its plain but fascinating chic. But she did know that Morton trusted her implicitly, and that made a pretty good basis for marriage, especially as they shared an interest in the fashion trade. It had always struck her as one of life's saddest sights to see people growing old alone. Martha, for instance, had never married. She had her sister's family, but no man of her own who had known her when she was young and lovely and who still retained that image of her.

After lunch she called Leigh and asked if they would be going to the party tonight. She knew Benji would be leaving early out of concern for his wife's condition and she could get a ride back with them in that case. But when Leigh said they were planning to have their own small celebration at home, Bliss asked if she might join them for a little while. "I've no taste for anything wet and noisy tonight," she explained.

"We'd love to have you, really! I want to show you what I've been knitting. It's getting terribly knotty. I keep forgetting what all those little abbreviations mean and having to go back to the front of the book. Do you know anything about knitting?"

Bliss didn't know much, but she could follow instructions well enough to get along, and so she promised to be there shortly after dinner, refusing an invitation to join them for that.

Later, wrapped in her dressing gown, she fingered the bronze that Morton had wanted her to wear. It was a gorgeous thing, really, but she knew she would never wear it again. It reminded her of the unfortunate episode with Bruce Pittmann. Instead, she selected a long patterned velvet skirt in shades of blue and turquoise with a tracery of black and wore it with a black silk turtleneck top. It was flattering and festive, and she felt like honoring the occasion for some reason. She didn't plan to stay late, for they would probably want to toast the New Year alone with each other, but it might give a bit of a lift in case either of them felt neglected for having to avoid the crush. She would take along a tin of the cheese biscuits she had made and a bottle of Morton's best champagne.

Morton looked exceedingly handsome and more flamboyant than usual in his dark maroon suit. He greeted her coolly. "I called Benji to wish him happy and he asked me to ask you to please bring along a bottle." He lifted his quizzical eyebrows and gave her a slightly hurt look.

"Oh, Morton, darling . . . I told you I didn't really want to go to this thing tonight. You know the real reason, too, so don't pretend with me. I thought Benji and Leigh could do with a spot of cheering up since they can't go out." She put her hands on his shoulders and gave him a look that begged indulgence.

"If I remember correctly, Benji's celebration last year lasted about thirty-six hours," he said disparagingly. And then, with a rather bleak warmth creeping into his tired eyes: "All right, my dear. I won't ask what happened last night between you and James, but just remember this . . . I love you very much." He held her close for an instant, then kissed her very tenderly on her lips. When he released her, allowing his shoulders to droop rather tiredly, he looked every one of his forty-six years. "You'll always have a place here, Bliss, no matter what."

For a few minutes after he had gone, Bliss stood

there, fighting an impulse to call him back and say she would go with him. Why was it that the more one loved, the more one ached? There were times when she thought the whole matter of loving a highly overrated affair.

And then she stirred herself; Morton would be picking up Adela and the two of them could well do without a third, no matter how fond they were of that third. And now, if she hoped to get a cab anytime tonight, she had better get cracking. There would be more than one person in London tonight who considered it wise to allow a professional to do the driving. Not that she planned to do much celebrating, but two glasses of champagne tended to render her more or less incompetent and there was no use courting disaster.

While she waited, she thumbed through one of Morton's glossy fashion magazines. Her mind moved on from the picture of a tall, blond model to wonder what Rona would be wearing tonight and whether or not James would take her home with him after the party. If he did, she probably wouldn't be shown to a rose and green and ivory room, but would be invited to make herself at home on a celadon bed in a room of tobacco brown and white.

The thought brought a sharp pain to her heart. She flung down the magazine and crossed the room restlessly to stare out into the night, seeing to the south of her the festive glow of lights radiating into a misty, frosty sky.

Both Leigh and Benji were dressed for the occasion, with Leigh sporting a sequined maternity suit that had the reverse effect of making her look younger than ever. The three of them sat around the crowded little room sipping on the chilled champagne that Benji had produced as Bliss had handed over her own offering. "I'll put this in for the next celebration. Morton was by earlier and left this."

She stayed for perhaps an hour and a half, warming herself by the glow of love that flowed so readily between them, and then she made a move to go. "If you'll call me a cab, Benji, I may manage to be out of your hair by midnight." She laughed. "Just think, next year this time, you'll be wanting to shush all the horns and hooters before they wake the baby."

The call was never made, though, for just as Benji rose to go to the phone, the doorbell sounded and he changed direction to admit James, bearing his own offering of champagne.

After greetings were over, Bliss made a move toward the phone, gathering up her coat as she went. She would wait out on the doorstep rather than in this closely confined space, as nothing seemed to lessen the effect James had on her body's chemistry. It was as if he carried with him some strange magnetic field and every time she came within range of him every ion of her being was drawn inexorably into his potent spell.

"Not leaving already, are you?" he queried, accepting one of her cheese biscuits from Leigh.

She nodded, not trusting herself to speak at first. "I'm afraid I'll outstay my welcome," she managed with a small laugh.

"I doubt it. Stick around a little longer. I thought this might be a good time to tell them about . . ." He gave her a significant look and she dropped down onto the straight chair beside the door.

After the next few minutes, another bottle of

champagne was called for. Bliss felt almost as tearful as Leigh, and they laughed with a newfound warmth as the men pretended to a greater stoicism, but there was no disguising the fact that the news had bowled them over.

There was another rush of conversation, with Leigh trying to remember the details of a house she had seen only once, several years earlier, and Benji wanting to know all about the neighborhood and details of commuting. Bliss had realized for some time that the house was the one James had bought for himself and Celine, and she couldn't think of a nicer way to exorcise old ghosts.

Finally, reluctantly, she stood up. "I must get a cab before the real rush begins. Darned if I want to have to sleep in the crib in your spare room!"

"I'll drive you home," James told her firmly. "You'll never even get a call through tonight, much less secure a ride."

She was disgusted at the surge of excitement she felt at his words, and when they left just before midnight, leaving the two newlyweds to usher in the New Year in their own fashion, she acted far more cool than she was feeling. About halfway between the Paddington flat and Morton's house, the chimes began to peal and then there was a blare of horns. James pulled over to the curb, switching off the engine.

"I've no more champagne in my pocket, but I can think of an even nicer way to usher in the New Year," he said softly in the warm darkness of the interior of his car.

"I . . . oh . . . Happy New Year, James," she said breathlessly, eyeing him warily.

He reached across and pulled her to him, bridging

the space between the seats as if it didn't exist. "I can think of more comfortable spots for this, but under the circumstances . . ." His mouth found her own and he proceeded to kiss her with a thoroughness that left her gasping helplessly. "Happy New Year, my dear," he whispered, holding her face in his two hands. She could barely see the outline of his features but her fingers lifted with unerring accuracy to trace the line between his lips.

He caught her fingertip in his teeth, nipping, then kissing, and when she felt the electrifying touch of his tongue on her flesh, she braced herself and said with scarcely a tremor, "Happy New Year, James. You're really an awfully nice man, no matter what."

He laughed, and the sound was more felt than heard. "I'm not sure I care much for the qualification," he said, still holding her hand captive and leaving a kiss in her palm.

"You know what I mean," she murmured, her mind scarcely functioning as the demands of her body threatened to overcome her reason.

"I'm not sure I do. You don't care for me very much, do you, Bliss?"

She pulled away, but he didn't let her go far, retaining a hold on her upper arms and keeping her turned toward him. "You don't trust me, do you, Bliss Bonner?" It was more a statement than a question.

"Trust has nothing to do with it. I . . . It's just . . . well, certainly I like you well enough, and what you did tonight was simply grand, but I . . . I really don't know you very well, James."

"Would you care to know me better, then?"

It was a dare, one she wanted with all her heart to accept but was afraid to risk. When she didn't answer, he pulled her back into his arms and buried his face in the fragrance of her hair. "Come to the party with me, hmmm?" he demanded, running a hand under her short coat to trace the hollow of her spine.

"No. I don't want to go, but you go on. I'm sure Rona is growing impatient, waiting for you." Her voice was colored by her feeling of bitterness, but she couldn't help it.

"You don't care very much for Rona, do you?"

She moved his hand away from her midriff where he had been toying with her waistband. "I neither like nor dislike her," she stated succinctly. "I think we'd better move on. It's already next year."

"So it is, so it is. Well, Bliss Bonner, before I return to the fray, I intend to give you something to think about for the next week or so." And before she could avoid him, he had turned her to him and was threatening the very air in her lungs by the force of his embrace. When his mouth covered hers with a kiss that demanded every last vestige of her soul, she offered it up freely, totally, unable to hold back anything of herself.

His hands made free of her body, caressing and exploring. When he cupped her breast tenderly, she caught at his hand and pressed it against her fiercely.

"Put your hands inside my shirt, darling," he whispered hoarsely against her mouth. "I want to feel your hands on my body." He groaned when her fingers fumbled clumsily with the hard front of his shirt, finding studs that refused to be released and he cursed softly when he struck the gearshift with his arm. "Bliss," he agonized, "I'll be in no shape to go to any party tonight."

The words struck her like a blast of Arctic air and

she stilled. How could he sit here in a parked car, making love her her like some fervid adolescent, while all the time he was wondering how he was going to explain his dishevelment to Rona?

"That's enough, James," she said with a determination she dredged up from some untapped resource. "I think we'd better go home now."

"You're right, of course. This is neither the time nor the place. I'll take you home, then, Bliss. I wish I could come in for a nightcap, but I really do have a commitment to honor."

"I don't recall inviting you," she said coolly, rebuttoning the coat that she seemed to have shed during the past few minutes.

He took her to the door, and when she turned to thank him for bringing her home, he caught her to him and kissed her briefly, but hard, very hard. "I'll be flying to the States first thing tomorrow for perhaps a week. I'll call as soon as I get back. Meanwhile, try and keep those two youngsters from breaking their necks out at Mallows, will you? I want to have a team in to go over everything before they move a stick of furniture."

Wordlessly, she nodded, feeling a coldness creeping over her that had nothing at all to do with the chill of the night.

Chapter Ten

Morning brought the familiar sounds and scents: coffee and bacon, Martha singing in the kitchen to signal that it was time for everyone to be up and about, Morton's electric shaver humming like an aroused hornet and the creaking of the central heating unit as it gathered its forces for an assault on the night's cold temperatures.

Bliss rolled over and wondered why her morning looked so gloomy in spite of a slice of cobalt sky showing through the open draperies, and then it all came back to her—James was gone. He would be gone for ages and there was no guarantee, in spite of his casual mention of a call, that he would get in touch with her on his return. He might be in London for weeks before she even knew it, and she had already had a preview of the sort of agony in store for her.

Forcing an indifferent body into action, she showered and pulled on a one-piece jump suit of gray tweed that had been a mistake as far as color was concerned. It only emphasized the pallor of her face and the shadows beneath her finely drawn cheekbones. When she and Morton stared at each other across the breakfast table, both grimaced and reached for the coffeepot.

"You look slightly hung over," she observed wryly. It was true, to her surprise. Morton, as a rule, was as conservative in his drinking habits as in all else.

"You don't exactly look like an advertisement for good cheer yourself. James said he brought you home from Benji's at a reasonable hour, so it must be dyspepsia."

"I think it's dry rot. A sort of January deterioration that makes me restless for spring," she murmured, spooning another heap of brown sugar into her already sweetened coffee. "Maybe it's time for a change, Morton," she declared, realizing the truth of her half-joking words even as she heard herself speak them.

"Not you, too! Adela mentions going back to Paris to renew herself, Rona talks about going home to get her future in shape . . . next thing we know, Martha will be making plans to move to the south of France and open up a tearoom."

"Oh, Lord, I hope not!" Bliss exclaimed, wrinkling her nose at the syrupy coffee. "What did you mean about Rona?" she asked curiously.

He shrugged. "Oh, nothing specific. Just that she mentioned last night when I said something about lunch this week that she would be flying home today, and when I asked if she plans on coming back, she gave one of her slow, sleepy smiles and told me

Adela was looking for me." He pushed away his half-empty plate. "Ah, well . . . she was half my age and I didn't really fancy her all that much. Flattered, I suppose, like any other old fool. It takes more than money and congenital low blood pressure to keep up with your generation, I'm afraid."

He gave her a smile that held traces of warmth, affection and a rueful sort of self-amusement. Bliss reached across the table and squeezed his hand, not trusting herself to speak at the moment.

James and Rona. No wonder he had been in such a hurry to get back last night! Certain commitments he had to honor, he had said, and she, like the fool she was, had been half convinced that she was coming to mean more to him than just another willing female, another conquest to be enjoyed for a few weeks and then tossed aside to make way for the next contender.

"By the way, James said he'd told the children about the house. I must say, I think he's been damned good about the whole thing, considering his opinion of Benji . . . not that he wasn't justified in what he thought. They've both come about one hundred and eighty degrees since then, haven't they?" He stood up and dusted crumbs from his flawlessly tailored flannels. "Going to lend a hand in the refurbishing? Right up your alley, I'd say. You always did enjoy messing about the house more than you did anything I could offer, more's the pity."

"You offered me the house, too, Morton. Everything I have I owe to you, dear, and I'm feeling an ungrateful wretch because now I'm suddenly wondering if it's enough."

He sat down again and looked at her steadily across the table. "No, love, of course it isn't enough.

I've never deluded myself that I could keep you forever . . . at least not in some years. If you feel the urge to strike out on your own, I'll help in any way I can. I've a few contacts in that business world you so deplore, you know . . . one or two in the decorating field. You've a definite flair for it."

The idea had been hovering in the fringes of her mind lately, if only because it was the one thing she was faintly interested in doing. But she knew she really wanted to spend her time and energies decorating and maintaining a home for herself and some man who would be content to allow her to baby him and pander to him in exchange for the same sort of treatment for herself.

Bah! Best get rid of any such notions of romantic drivel right now . . . nip them in the bud! In this day and age, that sort of marriage just didn't happen!

Unbidden, the image of Benji and Leigh arose in her mind's eye and she pushed it away. "I think I'll run back out to Mallows just to have a look around," she told Morton. "There might be a few things in the attic here that would help fill all those empty rooms, if you don't mind."

He nodded, shrugging into his chesterfield and brushing a kiss across her cheek on his way out. "Don't linger too long, though. There's no heat in the place and you tend to get carried away when you sink your teeth into some new project. I'll be spending the day with Adela . . . warding off home-sickness so she won't up and leave me with no manager," he explained with a half-rueful smile.

Bliss arrived to find the house wide open and swarming with carpenters and cleaners, which was just as well, considering that she didn't have a key.

That was remedied almost immediately, however, when one of the workmen, whose name was Mac-Nab and who designated himself foreman, handed her a ring with several keys on it.

"The housing agent said the Etchison bloke wants you to have this. Says you'll be here off and on and we're to listen to whatever notion takes yer fancy."

His expression gave Bliss a clue to just how welcome any suggestions from her might be, and she contented herself with wandering about, generally getting in the way, as she tried to envision the home that would evolve from all the noisy coming and going, hammering and sawing. When she walked in on a string of profanity that would have done credit to Liverpool's finest, she opted for the garden, despite the raw wind and dropping temperatures.

Work gloves would have been nice as it was physically impossible for her to spend more than five minutes in an overgrown garden without getting involved. By the time the workmen took a lunch break, she had cleared away an invasion of ground ivy, staked up several vines for future handling and made a start toward clearing out dead canes from among the ramblers.

When the workmen took their pasties and ale out onto the sunny side porch, she strolled through to find that the cleaners had already finished the downstairs and gone for the day and there were signs of repairs well under way throughout. Some of the wall colors, although freshly scrubbed, were rather ghastly. But she decided Leigh would be the one to choose the colors she would be living with. It wouldn't do to be thought a meddling sister-in-law, not when they were getting along so well these days.

All in all, she came three times that week, and by

the time the workmen were done she was on a first-name basis with all except for the feisty little Mr. MacNab, who insisted on the dignity of his station. He had done something noisy and esoteric with the plumbing and pronounced it shipshape and Bristol fashion, and when they took their leave that last afternoon, he had come close to bowing, with a superb flick of his battered bowler.

The garden was beginning to look as hopeful as a garden can in January. As long as the weather held dry, she could hope to get it cleared away so that when things began to sprout in the spring, Leigh would have some inkling of what was what and where.

Meanwhile, there was one last labor of love to be done and she was glad to have the place to herself for a change. On a Sunday morning when Morton announced that he was going to be closeted with Adela and would probably be late, since they were well into the spring season as far as fashion was concerned, Bliss set forth with her gardening tools and a box of carefully selected settings of winter heath. It was a ridiculous time of year to be planting them, but she was determined that next winter, when the snow was on the ground, Leigh and Benji would be able to look out their breakfast-room window and see a rosy blush of blossoms to remind them that no matter how long the winter, spring always comes. She had swaths of both rose and white in Morton's garden, and later on she would transplant more for them, if she was around.

That was another reason for her restless feeling of urgency. Who knew where she would be in another year? Certainly somewhere where she wouldn't be apt to run into James.

And thinking of James, as she did more hours than she cared to acknowledge, that was another good thing that had come from the week of hard work at Mallows. She had exorcised a number of ghosts and now she felt certain that if she could make it until she found herself a niche somewhere out of London, she would be well on the road to recovery by the time another season rolled around.

By lunchtime, she had cleared the patch where she meant to plant the heather. It was atop a rock-walled corner of the garden in what had probably once been a compost heap which had long since gone to earth. Now, with the weeds scraped away and the rocks cleared of trailing vines, she poured herself a cup of tea from her flask and surveyed the situation.

It was almost warm here in the sunshine, and she pulled off her anorak and unbuttoned the top button of her shirt, feeling the icy touch of air on her damp throat. Her nails would never be the same, and when she pushed her hair from her face, she left a smudge of dirt. But she was too intent on visualizing the best arrangement to even think of how she looked.

By the time the last tender shoot was embedded in the rich loam, she breathed a sigh of pure satisfaction and moved backward so that she was perched on the very edge of the four-foot-tall rock wall. A low border, perhaps one that trailed down among the rocks, would be nice later on, and she was mentally selecting and discarding from among several possibilities when she heard a footstep behind her. In her precarious position, she could only twist her head around, and before she could complete the move, she heard a familiar baritone bark out her name.

"Bliss!"

The next thing she knew, she was on her back on the ground with her feet still propped up on the wall and James's dark, grim face was leaning over her.

"What the hell do you think you were doing?" he demanded, his hands going over her as if to check for broken bones.

"Thanks, I'm fine, and how are you?" she asked sarcastically, stretching a limb experimentally.

When he held out a hand she ignored it, rolling over to her knees and pulling herself up by a handful of rough, lichen-covered rocks. She was beginning to feel the jolt her back had taken. That, plus the fact that he had come upon her looking like a scarecrow, made her temper rise rapidly to the boiling point. It was his fault she had taken a tumble in the first place, coming up behind her like that, and she told him as much.

"My fault!" he exploded. "I suppose I ordered you to go crawling around on rock walls backwards with a lethal weapon in your hand! I suppose I ordered you to come out here every day and work yourself to the bone doing what I hired someone to do next week!"

She glared down at the trowel she was holding defensively and taken back up into his gloriously, wonderfully furious face. "Well, you sneaked up behind me and yelled at me and made me fall! How was I to know you were anywhere in the country? For all I knew you were paddling your canoe down the Potomac with your banjo on your knee!"

His eyes closed momentarily and a muscle in his jaw quivered. "You don't know a lot about the States, do you? Come on, get in the house now and let me look you over for damage. You're an earthy little creature, aren't you, for all the occasional glamour?" He took her arm and propelled her in through the garden door. Then, when they were inside, out of the wind, he took her by the shoulders, turned her to face him and slowly considered every inch of her, from head to toe. By the time he had completed the survey, she felt as if her bones had melted like candle wax, leaving her without support for the bundle of nerves that were beginning to quiver under his touch.

His eyes tangled with her own and held them there. When he spoke, she was listening with her body instead of her mind. "You've a smudge on your face," he told her.

She lifted a hand slowly and it hovered somewhere in the vicinity of her cheek. "What face?" she asked, bemused.

His eyes crinkled at her, and for the first time she noticed how much paler he looked, almost gaunt. "Have you been ill?" she asked.

"No, I haven't been ill. What I have been is without sleep for the past thirty-six hours or thereabouts. Speaking of looking ill, what have you been doing to yourself? Aside from the obvious?"

"Well, for one thing, I've been improving your property," she retorted.

"You certainly haven't been improving yourself. You look like the very devil!"

"How kind of you to say so," she replied with saccharine sweetness.

"Nor have you been improving your disposition."

"Well, what do you expect when you come knocking me off walls and telling me how terrible I look?" she demanded unreasonably.

"Well, what do *you* expect when I spend thirty-six

hours racing my fool head off to get to some idiot of a woman who hasn't got the sense to know—"

Stung by his exasperated outburst, Bliss broke in to ask sarcastically, "And where *is* Rona? Don't tell me you left her to freeze out in the car?"

His frown grew even stormier. "Rona? She's home as far as I know. Why?"

"You mean back in the States?" Bliss blinked.

"As far as I know she hasn't taken out British citizenship."

"There's a much quicker way to gain British citizenship," she muttered, glaring down at her filthy hands and frowning at her broken nails.

He jerked her face up with an ungentle hand beneath her chin. "Just what are you going on about?"

She faced him down belligerently, her wide, slightly nearsighted eyes daring him to offer sympathy. "You left with her, didn't you? January first . . . a few hours after you dropped me off to go back to her party? It's pretty obvious. . . ."

"Nothing is obvious, you silly dunce! If you've missed what's as plain as the dirt on your face, then nothing at *all* is obvious!" He shook her impatiently and pulled her into his arms, dirt, tattered work clothes and all. "Woman, what am I going to do with you?"

With a new hope rising tremulously in her like the sun breaking through the clouds, she whispered, "What do you want to do with me?"

From where she stood, with her face held tightly against his chest, Bliss could see the pulse that jumped under his jaw. When he told her just what he wanted to do with her, his voice sounded as unsteady as her legs felt.

"But that'll have to wait a few days," he added. "No longer than it takes to get your name on the license and say our bit before the preacher."

His heart was thundering now beneath her head and she pulled away to stare up at him. There were things she had to know and it was a fair certainty that they wouldn't be talking much longer.

When James took her hand, garden soil and all, and began to kiss each separate finger, Bliss made a fist. "James, you can't do that," she protested, aghast.

"Seems to me I just did," he observed mildly. Then, pulling her off balance so that she fell against him, he tightened his arms and growled against her ear, "I guess it's a case of love me, love my dirt. I do, you know."

A vast cavern opened up in the region where her heart once was. "You do . . . what?" she whispered.

"You know very well what I do. Haven't I just gotten through proposing to you? Do you think I could make love to a slip of a girl with dirty hands and face unless I loved her to distraction and back again?"

She wrapped her arms around his waist and squeezed, wishing she could get closer to him. "I wish you wouldn't keep on about my dirty hands," she whispered. "I do have my cleaner moments, you know."

"Are you going to put me out of my misery, sweetheart?"

"I don't know what you're talking about," she parried, still unable to believe in what was happening.

"Don't play games, Bliss," he said deeply. "One

186

of the things I love about you is that you don't play games . . . of any sort. Even with poor old Reade, it was more a case of omission than commission, I suspect, that got you almost to the point of no return."

"You've been there, too, James. Was that one or the other?" She meant with Celine, but it was Rona he spoke of.

"It was neither, I'm afraid. Purely a case of self-defense. I found myself falling in love against all my better judgment and I ran as fast as I could in the opposite direction . . . which, in this case, happened to be Rona MacMurdle. It could as easily have been Celine Thomas or any one of half a dozen other women who've passed through my life without making a dent." He placed a finger across her lips when she would have argued with him. "Ah-ah. Before you start reading me chapter and verse of my lurid past, let me assure you that what once passed for love in my life was a combination of convenience, conditions and, I'm afraid, pure boredom. I was fed up with the shallowness of my social life and when someone attractive offered a change, I couldn't come up with a single reason why not."

Bliss rather thought there had been more to it than that, but the past was done with and before them was a future that was only beginning to hint at the wonders it held. She ran her hands inside his coat and traced the hollow of his spine as far as she could reach. "James . . . when did it start . . . for you?" she asked shyly.

With his heart thundering so that his voice shook just a bit, he told her. "I had seen you with Morton enough to know who you were, and with Johnston enough to confuse the issue. Then, when I mistook a trip to the dentist for the remnants of a night of celebration, I was very nearly fit to be tied, without ever wondering why. I think it was at the cottage when I began to suspect you were going to play a major part in my future, either that or I was going to have to . . ." He laughed shakily and Bliss stood on tiptoe to bury her face in his warm throat.

"Oh, darling, if you only knew what I've been going through," she whispered, feeling ridiculous tears flowing up from the depths of her. "The very first time I saw you you made me mad as could be, and from then on, I was always far too conscious of you to behave rationally. That day we met at lunch with Morton and Leigh . . . I felt as if something momentous had happened to me, but it was not until much later that I realized what it was. It was as if," she confided, leaning back to blink up at him, "I'd been asleep forever and was just waking up."

"Lord, darling, don't cry! We'll have mud everywhere." He touched her face with the tip of a finger and lifted a tear from her cheek. "Did you know I've been chasing you through at least a dozen lifetimes? Now that I've finally caught up with you, we're going to have quite a lot of catching up to do." He touched her lips with his, then lifted them, and with a groan, he captured her mouth in a kiss that held all the longing, all the frustration and the eagerness of a lifetime of searching. "Let's get out of here, darling," he whispered. "You're going to have to have a bath or two, and I'm going to have to have a nap. I'm warning you, I have no intention of letting you out of my sight for at least the next five years, so on our way back home, you can try and figure that one out, hmmm?"

IT'S YOUR OWN SPECIAL TIME

Contemporary romances for today's women.
Each month, six very special love stories will be yours
from SILHOUETTE. Look for them wherever books are sold
or order now from the coupon below.

$1.50 each

__# 1 PAYMENT IN FULL Hampson
__# 2 SHADOW AND SUN Carroll
__# 3 AFFAIRS OF THE HEART Powers
__# 4 STORMY MASQUERADE Hampson
__# 5 PATH OF DESIRE Goforth
__# 6 GOLDEN TIDE Stanford
__# 7 MIDSUMMER BRIDE Lewis
__# 8 CAPTIVE HEART Beckman
__# 9 WHERE MOUNTAINS WAIT Wilson
__#10 BRIDGE OF LOVE Caine
__#11 AWAKEN THE HEART Vernon
__#12 UNREASONABLE SUMMER Browning
__#13 PLAYING FOR KEEPS Hastings
__#14 RED, RED ROSE Oliver
__#15 SEA GYPSY Michaels
__#16 SECOND TOMORROW Hampson
__#17 TORMENTING FLAME John
__#18 THE LION'S SHADOW Hunter
__#19 THE HEART NEVER FORGETS Thornton
__#20 ISLAND DESTINY Fulford
__#21 SPRING FIRES Richards
__#22 MEXICAN NIGHTS Stephens
__#23 BEWITCHING GRACE Edwards
__#24 SUMMER STORM Healy
__#25 SHADOW OF LOVE Stanford
__#26 INNOCENT FIRE Hastings
__#27 THE DAWN STEALS SOFTLY Hampson
__#28 MAN OF THE OUTBACK Hampson
__#29 RAIN LADY Wildman
__#30 RETURN ENGAGEMENT Dixon

__#31 TEMPORARY BRIDE Halldorson
__#32 GOLDEN LASSO Michaels
__#33 A DIFFERENT DREAM Vitek
__#34 THE SPANISH HOUSE John
__#35 STORM'S END Stanford
__#36 BRIDAL TRAP McKay
__#37 THE BEACHCOMBER Beckman
__#38 TUMBLED WALL Browning
__#39 PARADISE ISLAND Sinclair
__#40 WHERE EAGLES NEST Hampson
__#41 THE SANDS OF TIME Owen
__#42 DESIGN FOR LOVE Powers
__#43 SURRENDER IN PARADISE Robb
__#44 DESERT FIRE Hastings
__#45 TOO SWIFT THE MORNING Carroll
__#46 NO TRESPASSING Stanford
__#47 SHOWERS OF SUNLIGHT Vitek
__#48 A RACE FOR LOVE Wildman
__#49 DANCER IN THE SHADOWS Wisdom
__#50 DUSKY ROSE Scott
__#51 BRIDE OF THE SUN Hunter
__#52 MAN WITHOUT A HEART Hampson
__#53 CHANCE TOMORROW Browning
__#54 LOUISIANA LADY Beckman
__#55 WINTER'S HEART Ladame
__#56 RISING STAR Trent
__#57 TO TRUST TOMORROW John
__#58 LONG WINTER'S NIGHT Stanford
__#59 KISSED BY MOONLIGHT Vernon
__#60 GREEN PARADISE Hill

___ #61 WHISPER MY NAME Michaels
___ #62 STAND-IN BRIDE Halston
___ #63 SNOWFLAKES IN THE SUN Brent
___ #64 SHADOW OF APOLLO Hampson
___ #65 A TOUCH OF MAGIC Hunter
___ #66 PROMISES FROM THE PAST Vitek
___ #67 ISLAND CONQUEST Hastings
___ #68 THE MARRIAGE BARGAIN Scott
___ #69 WEST OF THE MOON St. George
___ #70 MADE FOR EACH OTHER Afton Bonds
___ #71 A SECOND CHANCE ON LOVE Ripy
___ #72 ANGRY LOVER Beckman
___ #73 WREN OF PARADISE Browning
___ #74 WINTER DREAMS Trent
___ #75 DIVIDE THE WIND Carroll
___ #76 BURNING MEMORIES Hardy
___ #77 SECRET MARRIAGE Cork
___ #78 DOUBLE OR NOTHING Oliver
___ #79 TO START AGAIN Halldorson

___ #80 WONDER AND WILD DESIRE Stephens
___ #81 IRISH THOROUGHBRED Roberts
___ #82 THE HOSTAGE BRIDE Dailey
___ #83 LOVE LEGACY Halston
___ #84 VEIL OF GOLD Vitek
___ #85 OUTBACK SUMMER John
___ #86 THE MOTH AND THE FLAME Adams
___ #87 BEYOND TOMORROW Michaels
___ #88 AND THEN CAME DAWN Stanford
___ #89 A PASSIONATE BUSINESS James
___ #90 WILD LADY Major
___ #91 WRITTEN IN THE STARS Hunter
___ #92 DESERT DEVIL McKay
___ #93 EAST OF TODAY Browning
___ #94 ENCHANTMENT Hampson
___ #95 FOURTEEN KARAT BEAUTY Wisdom
___ #96 LOVE'S TREACHEROUS JOURNEY Beckman
___ #97 WANDERER'S DREAM Clay
___ #98 MIDNIGHT WINE St. George
___ #99 TO HAVE, TO HOLD Camp

$1.75 each

___ # 100 YESTERDAY'S SHADOW Stanford
___ # 101 PLAYING WITH FIRE Hardy
___ # 102 WINNER TAKE ALL Hastings
___ # 103 BY HONOUR BOUND Cork
___ # 104 WHERE THE HEART IS Vitek
___ # 105 MISTAKEN IDENTITY Eden
___ # 109 FIRE UNDER SNOW Vernon
___ # 110 A STRANGER'S WIFE Trent
___ # 111 WAYWARD LOVER South

___ # 106 THE LANCASTER MEN Dailey
___ # 107 TEARS OF MORNING Bright
___ # 108 FASCINATION Hampson
___ # 112 WHISPER WIND Stanford
___ # 113 WINTER BLOSSOM Browning
___ # 114 PAINT ME RAINBOWS Michaels
___ # 115 A MAN FOR ALWAYS John
___ # 116 AGAINST THE WIND Lindley
___ # 117 MANHATTAN MASQUERADE Scott

Silhouette Romance

15-Day Free Trial Offer
6 Silhouette Romances

6 Silhouette Romances, free for 15 days! We'll send you 6 new Silhouette Romances to keep for 15 days, absolutely free! If you decide not to keep them, send them back to us. You pay nothing.

Free Home Delivery. But if you enjoy them as much as we think you will, keep them by paying the invoice enclosed with your free trial shipment. We'll pay all shipping and handling charges. You get the convenience of Home Delivery and we pay the postage and handling charge each month.

Don't miss a copy. The Silhouette Book Club is the way to make sure you'll be able to receive every new romance we publish before they're sold out. There is no minimum number of books to buy and you can cancel at any time.